MW01126447

RECKONING

DARK ROAD – BOOK SIX

BRUNO MILLER

RECKONING:
Dark Road, Book Six

Copyright © 2019 Bruno Miller

All rights reserved. No part of this book may be reproduced in any form or by any electronic or mechanical means, including information storage and retrieval systems—except in the case of brief quotations embodied in critical articles or reviews—without permission in writing from the author.

This book is a work of fiction. The characters, events, and places portrayed in this book are products of the author's imagination and are either fictitious or are used fictitiously. Any similarity to real person, living or dead, is purely coincidental and not intended by the author.

Find out when Bruno's next book is coming out. Join his mailing list for release news, sales, and the occasional survival tip. No spam ever. http://brunomillerauthor.com/sign-up/

Published in the United States of America.

Will you be ready when the reckoning comes?

After a grueling trip, Ben, Joel, Allie, her mother Sandy, and Gunner have reached their destination on the Eastern shore of Maryland.

Ben is reunited with his two younger children who have been surviving with the help of their ailing grandfather, Jack and his dog Sam. But reaching Jack's farm doesn't guarantee their safety, however, and the struggle to survive continues.

They must remain vigilant in their efforts to protect what is theirs, and the people they love. Ben is hoping for a chance to re-supply and get some much needed rest after their cross country ordeal, but fate has other plans for them.

Jack's stubbornness in accepting help and refusal to leave his farm means Ben must make a tough decision about doing what's best for his children. They're forced to prepare quickly for the journey back to Colorado. But will they all make it home?

THE DARK ROAD SERIES

· 1 ·

As the realization that they had finally made it to Maryland sunk in, Ben began to relax for the first time in a while. It was a long, grueling trip, longer than he anticipated, and much of it was a struggle to simply survive. But seeing his kids together again made it all worthwhile, and reuniting Allie with her mother was the icing on the cake. Although life as they knew it was in chaos, Ben was content with the fact that he had all his kids under one roof again.

The trip had exhausted them all, including Gunner, who was sprawled out on the tile floor in Jack's kitchen. Allie and her mother had gone upstairs to get cleaned up for dinner, but Allie was the only one to return. Sandy had fallen asleep while waiting for Allie to finish, and Ben didn't blame her for it one bit. It was likely the first time she'd enjoyed the luxury of a real bed since the EMPs hit. Not even the promise of a hot meal was tempting enough to lure her back downstairs or out of bed.

Allie apologized for her mother falling asleep so quickly, but no one faulted her for it. Ben imagined that Sandy's struggles over the last several days had really taken a toll on her health and mental well-being. She had probably assumed her daughter was gone. That would be enough to break most people, but she had pushed onward and hadn't given up. Ben admired her for that and could see now where Allie got her drive and perseverance.

As they all sat down at the table, Ben looked around at his children. It was still hard to believe that they were all in one place and together again. He hated to admit it, but on more than one occasion over the last week or so, he doubted he would ever see this moment. When he looked back on the trip here, it seemed almost impossible that they made it to Jack's at all. All that they had seen and been through in the few days since they left Colorado felt impossible to Ben.

But it was real, and they were all finally here, safe and sound. He had his kids back under his watchful eye once more, and for the first time since the journey began, he felt like he was in control of their destiny. The world outside the door might disagree with his plans for everyone, but for right now, none of that mattered.

Jack returned from the kitchen with a pitcher of iced tea he'd made from the water they boiled on the grill. Jack said it was best to make tea out of the water to help hide its unusual taste, but Ben wasn't expecting actual ice in it.

"Is that ice?" Joel asked.

"Sure is. I've got a small countertop icemaker that I run when the generator's going. It cycles through pretty quick and makes about a pound of ice every fifteen minutes. That's how I'm able to keep the venison from going bad. Been using the big chest freezer in the outbuilding like a big cooler."

Ben had noticed the meat on his plate but hadn't thought about the logistics behind the meal. Jack had a pretty good setup here, but it wouldn't sustain them with the addition of him, Joel, Allie, and her mom. Jack wanted them to stay for a while and recover from the trip, but Ben felt a little guilty about putting the extra burden on Jack and his resources.

"Oh, that's so good. It's been a long time since I've had an ice-cold drink." Allie held her glass with both hands as she savored the sweet tea. "I'm tempted to wake my mom up just for this."

"Let her sleep. There's plenty more where that came from," Jack replied. They all dug in as Gunner and Sam hovered around the table in the hope of receiving leftovers. The kids made small talk as they ate, and Joel and Allie fielded questions from Bradley and Emma about their adventure. They were sure to leave out some of the more gruesome details for the benefit of the younger kids, but Ben wondered if that was wise. They were only putting off the inevitable. Sooner or later, Bradley and Emma were going to have to see things for themselves. And they would no doubt see those things on the trip back to Colorado. There was no way to shelter them from the realities that lay ahead.

There was time to worry about that later. For now, Ben contented himself to sit back and listen to their stories. Occasionally, he caught himself staring at his two younger kids as if they would disappear any second. He and Jack could discuss the details of their return trip later. Right now, he just wanted to enjoy the moment while it lasted.

Ben also considered the possibility of trying to reason with Jack about him coming with them. He had broached the subject before dinner while they were outside, and Jack had given him a pretty firm answer. This was Jack's home, as it had been for the majority of his life, and while Ben understood his reluctance to leave, it didn't ease his conscience to think about leaving the old man behind.

How long could Jack survive here on his own? Was there more to his deteriorating health than he was letting on? Regardless of the real reason, Ben knew that staying here would mean certain death for Jack. The man was famously stubborn, though, and Ben feared that any further attempt to convince him otherwise would only push him further away. Ben tried to put himself in Jack's shoes and think about his reasoning.

Jack still had a daughter somewhere in all this craziness. The chance that Casey would ever return was slim, and regardless of what they told the kids, he and Jack both knew it. But as a father, he knew Jack wouldn't let go of that, no matter how small that sliver of hope was. Ben would easily do the same for any of his kids.

Right now, the kids seemed happy and secure in the fact that they had their father back, but the reality of losing their mother would settle in sooner or later. Maybe it already had, but Ben doubted it and assumed they were still in denial. He would have to deal with his ex's absence and its impact on the kids at some point down the road. Jack was pretty good at putting a positive spin on the situation and keeping their outlook optimistic, but that wouldn't last once they were on the road, although Ben wasn't sure how much of the act was for the kids' sake and how much Jack actually believed.

As everyone finished their dinner, Ben tried to put the negative thoughts out of his mind and live in the moment. He couldn't blame Jack for holding onto the possibility of Casey returning or trying to sugarcoat the reality of the situation for the kids' sake. Most people would have probably thought Ben was crazy for driving across the country to find Bradley and Emma. But they beat the odds and here they were. That was proof that anything was possible. Who was he to talk Jack out of staying behind for Casey's sake?

There wasn't much food left on anyone's plate, but there was a small amount left over that was meant for Sandy. Allie insisted on letting her sleep, and after checking in on her mother one more time, she gave the okay to share the leftovers with the two anxious dogs. Jack split the food equally over a serving of dry food and barely had a chance to set the bowls down before Gunner and Sam dove in. Both dogs licked the bowls clean, pushing them around the kitchen floor until they were spotless.

The kids retreated to the living room while Ben and Jack cleaned up. Allie offered to help, but Ben insisted that she go relax. He wanted his daughter and Allie to continue getting to know one another. She was a good role model for Emma, something his daughter could really benefit from right now.

Ben's ulterior motive for cleaning up without the kids was to get Jack alone again. Maybe he would talk more freely without the kids around and elaborate on what had been going on around here. Jack had mentioned some friends of his in town being threatened and leaving for North Carolina. How bad was it here, and would they have any trouble that Ben should be prepared for tonight?

· 2 ·

There was more that Jack wasn't letting on about the story, and Ben wondered if Jack was afraid to tell him the truth about the situation here. Maybe he feared that Ben and the kids would refuse to leave him behind if he was in danger.

Ben noticed a shotgun and hunting rifle by the door, and even in these circumstances, Jack wouldn't keep loaded guns lying around without good reason. He was far too safety-conscious for that, especially with the kids here, although both Bradley and Emma understood gun safety and knew how to shoot.

"Couldn't find a better spot, huh, guys?" Ben stepped over Gunner and Sam, who had both decided to lie in the doorway between the dining room and the kitchen.

"Always," Jack said. "Sam knows she'll get leftovers if she sticks around for clean-up."

Ben wasn't sure how to start the conversation and he wanted to tread lightly. "So how are you set on supplies? I mean, how long can you hold out and wait here for Casey?"

"If it's just me, I have all I need here for a long time. I've been using a lot of resources trying to keep things semi-normal for the kids. I don't need much to survive," Jack assured him.

"What about that trouble you mentioned closer into town? Any of that making its way out here?" Ben asked.

"A little, but we've been flying under the radar so far. I keep everything out of sight, and it doesn't hurt that this place doesn't exactly look like I have anything worth taking. Nobody pays attention to the house, and they pass us right by." Jack lit a lantern and set it on the kitchen table.

"Anything we should prepare for tonight? Should someone stay up and keep an eye on things?" Ben asked.

"No, it'll be fine once we shut down the generator and lock up," Jack said. Ben wasn't buying it and felt like he was only getting part of the story, but he didn't want to press him for any more information right now.

Maybe they hadn't had any real trouble yet, but he and Jack both knew it was only a matter of time. Out on the road, they'd seen too many examples of what people had resorted to in order to survive. This place was no different than any of the other places they'd passed through. Supplies were limited, and as resources continued to dwindle, someone would eventually notice the little yellow farmhouse. Or maybe Ben was just being paranoid.

"Speaking of locking up, you want to give me a hand out back?" Jack grabbed the five-gallon bucket he had been dumping ice into and started for the back entrance. Sam jumped up at the sound of the rear door opening and was eager to join the men outside. Gunner was much less enthusiastic and only lifted his head off the floor long enough to catch a glimpse of what was going on. Losing interest quickly, he rolled onto his side and spread out on the tile floor with a grunt. Content to be near the kids, he had no interest in joining Ben as he headed out.

Ben followed Jack and Sam outside, but instead of heading right for the outbuilding, Jack stopped on the deck and pulled a couple of cigars out of his shirt pocket. Jack didn't indulge often, but he did enjoy the occasional cigar. It was one of the things Ben remembered about duck hunting with him.

He offered one to Ben without saying anything. Ben wasn't a smoker by any means, but he took the cigar out of respect. It wouldn't hurt him to humor Jack, seeing as how it might be the last time the two of them had time together like this.

Jack used the lighter hanging off the grill to light Ben's cigar first. Then he lit his own before sauntering down the steps and out into the back yard. Sam was already on the ground and leisurely making her way around the yard, marking a few spots as she went. Jack took a couple of heavy puffs on his cigar and blew out a thick cloud of smoke.

"Nothing like a good cigar after a meal." Jack sighed as he made his way toward the outbuilding. Ben followed and drew in a mouthful of smoke, careful not to inhale any of it. The cigar was harsh and reminded him of the smells they encountered on the road and the burning towns they passed through. But if it made Jack happy and got him talking, Ben would play along.

"Hard to believe it's come to this, isn't it?" Ben said.

"Oh, I don't know. I think we've been headed down this path for some time now. I'm actually surprised it didn't happen sooner, to be honest." Jack shook his head. "Feel bad for the kids, though. They don't deserve this."

"No, they don't, and unfortunately, it's going to be up to them to clean up our mess."

"They've got a long road ahead of them." Jack looked off toward the horizon as the last bit of the setting sun disappeared behind the trees. Jack was right; it would take a long time for things to return to normal. And normal might not ever be what it once was. Ben preferred not to think of things on such a grand scale, although it was hard not to. Instead, he preferred to focus on the immediate future and their survival. That was the best way he could help his kids.

"Here, let me get that so you can get the door." Ben took the bucket of ice from Jack so he could use both hands to open the door, but he mostly took it because Jack looked like he was struggling with the weight of it. Jack was half the man Ben remembered, and he was reminded once again just how much time had passed since he'd last seen him. Sam noticed them heading into the garage and raced over so as to not be left out.

Jack led him to the chest freezer on the back wall. The lid creaked loudly as he lifted it for Ben to dump in the ice. Ben tried to do a quick assessment of the amount of food Jack had in there and was disappointed to see that it was less than a quarter full of small paper-wrapped packages that he presumed were venison. There was probably enough to last him three or four weeks if he was conservative. In Jack's physical condition, there was no way he was going to be able to hunt and restock the freezer with meat. He had the garden, which seemed to be thriving thanks to the pumped well water, but that wouldn't last past the fall, and the man couldn't live on vegetables alone, anyway.

Ben promised himself he wouldn't push Jack to come with them, but the thought of leaving him here to fend for himself was eating him up inside. It was a death sentence and Ben knew it. With the amount of supplies he had and his physical condition, Jack's fate would be sealed when they pulled out of here. Ben wasn't sure he could live with that on his conscience without trying to talk some sense into Jack at least one more time.

Jack pushed the ice around with his hand until it covered all the neatly wrapped packages of meat. Then he sprinkled salt over the whole thing.

"Come take a look at the Jeep." Jack pushed the freezer lid gently and let gravity do the rest as it slammed shut with a *thud*. Ben followed him over to the old Scrambler, where Jack proceeded to undo the hood latches. Sam stayed put this time, content to watch the men from her well-worn dog bed near the workbench.

"Take a look at that, will ya?" Jack propped the hood up and stepped back.

Ben was surprised at what he saw. The engine was spotless and looked to have all new parts and hoses attached as well.

"Wow, I didn't expect that." Ben admired the setup and couldn't help but put his hands on it. The engine block and valve cover were painted light blue and stood out against the bright-red sparkplug wires. It was very tidy, and Ben felt a sense of relief wash over him. He had been worried about the old Jeep making it back to Colorado, but not anymore.

"Complete replacement. I stuck with the 258 in-line six. She won't win any races, but I've got torque to spare. Pulls the boat with no problem," Jack boasted.

"Looks like you replaced everything," Ben said.

"Pretty much, and not just in here. I had the whole thing gone over mechanically. It might not look like much on the outside, but it's practically a new vehicle underneath. Spent just under eight grand makin' her right. Even put a new set of tires on."

Ben stepped back and looked at the aggressive thirty-five-inch all-terrain tires that fit snuggly under the fenders. The Jeep fit right in with the Blazer thanks to its homemade spray-painted camo paint job and oversized winch bumper, complete with LED off-road lights.

"I had to do something since it's my daily driver. Well, *was* my daily driver," Jack corrected himself.

"You must have had all this done recently?" Ben asked.

"About six months ago, right after I wrecked the Ford. She's only got eleven hundred miles on the new engine. Hardly even broke in yet." Jack started to lower the hood, and Ben gave him a hand closing it gently and latching it shut.

"We can't take it, Jack. We can't leave you stranded here." Ben was hit with a wave of guilt, and even at the risk of starting an argument, he thought it was as good a time as any to try talking

Jack into coming along one last time. The worst he could do was say no; then at least Ben would know he'd made every effort to reason with the man. He didn't want the image of Jack stuck here and wasting away gnawing at his conscience all the way back to Colorado. The trip would be stressful enough without the guilt. Jack's silence caught Ben off-guard, and all of a sudden, he felt awkward, like he'd opened a door he shouldn't have.

Jack took a puff on his cigar and slowly leaned back against the Jeep. For a minute, he had a faraway look in his eyes and seemed distracted. Ben stayed silent and made his way around the Jeep, inspecting the rest of the improvements as he went. He didn't regret asking Jack to come with them again—he didn't really have a choice if he was to have a chance at a clear conscience—but he didn't expect this reaction from Jack, either. The silence was so deafening that you could have heard a pin drop on the concrete floor. Finally, Jack straightened up as best as he could and Ben prepared himself for whatever news he was about to deliver.

"Ben, I can't go with you because... Well, because I haven't got long," Jack muttered.

"What do you mean?" Ben forgot all about the Jeep and feeling awkward.

Jack sighed. "I mean I'm dying, Ben. There's no other way to put it."

"Your heart?" Ben made his way to the hood of the truck so he could see Jack's face.

"No, I've got cancer. Well, I've got it again, actually. I went through chemotherapy a while back, and the doctor said I was good, but I went in for my yearly and they said it's back."

Ben had a heavy feeling in his stomach. "Casey never said anything about that. She told me you had heart trouble but it was under control with meds."

"I did have heart trouble. The chemo gave me arrhythmia. Believe me, it's been a tough couple years. Farthest I moved the boat last year was out of the garage for cleaning, and then it went back in. Only reason I have venison in the freezer is because I got lucky last year and took a deer from the porch with the rifle." Ben glanced over at the Blazer, which stood where the boat was normally parked. The shelves were loaded with hunting gear and duck decoys. He noticed a good layer of dust and cobwebs on just about everything.

"Yeah, I know it could use a little attention. Not exactly a high priority lately," Jack huffed.

It was as if a dark cloud had filled the room and Ben wasn't sure what to say next. He immediately thought of the kids and wondered if they knew that their grandfather was dying.

· 3 ·

Ben couldn't believe what he was hearing, but it began to make sense why Jack didn't want to come along and burden them. But still, Ben saw no reason to leave him here. At least he could be with family in his final days or weeks.

"You could still come with us. We can take care of you."

"Without treatment, they gave me a couple months or so. But that was a few weeks back, and I was supposed to start therapy the day after the EMPs hit. I'm going downhill fast, Ben. I can feel my strength fading a little more every day. I'm only hanging in there for the kids' sake, and I don't know how much longer I can keep it up." Jack paused to catch his breath and take another labored puff on the cigar. "I don't want them to know, to see me like this or how bad it's going to get."

"They have to know. Don't you think that's fair?" Ben asked.

"Fair?" Jack laughed. "The kids think I'm waiting here for Casey, and that's partially true, so I'd like to leave it at that. They don't need to know I'm dying. They've been through enough. Casey doesn't even know the cancer is back." Jack, an angry look on his face, pushed himself off the Jeep and slowly walked over to where Ben was standing. But as he approached, his face softened and he put his hand on Ben's shoulder.

"I can't tell you how happy I was to see you standing there on the front porch. I've been worried sick over the kids and what would happen to them if..." His eyes were red and glassy as he looked at Ben.

Jack nodded. "I've made peace with it. It's okay. And now that you're here, I can take comfort in the fact that they have you. I don't want to die out there in some strange place." Jack glanced over Ben's shoulder. "And I want the kids to remember me how I am—or how I was. I've made arrangements with the Smiths to bury me under the tree, if they're still around to do so."

Ben felt his throat tighten as Jack reasoned with him bluntly and explained the morbid details of his plan. He didn't want to accept it, but he would respect Jack's wishes. How could he argue with a dying man over his last request? To add insult to injury, he couldn't tell anyone the real reason why Jack wasn't coming with them.

He didn't think it was fair to leave the kids in the dark about something like that; he hated keeping information like this from them. In his mind, they deserved to know what was going on. They'd earned that much. It felt irresponsible to try and shield them from the truth. But this was his burden to bear now, and there was nothing he could do about it unless he disregarded Jack's wishes.

He wasn't sure how Bradley and Emma would take it, but he was positive that Joel would want to know and have the chance to say his final goodbyes to his grandfather. It would be hard, there was no denying that, but Ben had seen Joel—and Allie, for that matter—grow up a lot in the last couple of weeks. They'd both been dealt some blows along the way, yet they had never given in, at least not for long.

"I need to ask one more favor of you, Ben." Jack pulled back a little and looked toward the house.

"I'll do whatever you want." Ben's heart sank again. What was he going to ask him? *Dear Lord, please don't let him ask me to help him die,* Ben thought as he braced for the answer.

"Take Sam with you. She's got a few good years left in her. I don't want her to be here all alone when it happens. She should be with people she knows."

Ben nodded, relieved that Jack's request was an easy one. "Sure thing, Jack. No problem." Sam heard her name and her tail began to wag as she slowly got up and headed over to Jack, unaware that she'd just been given away.

"I owe her that much. She was always a good hunting partner and never let me down. You understand?" Jack grunted as he dropped to one knee and greeted Sam with a thorough head rub.

Jack stood up as fast as his old body would allow and started for the door. "Well, come on. Let's get back inside and lock up for the night. Tomorrow we've got a big day of sorting through gear and packing the Jeep."

"Good idea," Ben said. He followed Jack outside and helped him with the bucket and the lantern as he locked the outbuilding doors. Ben didn't want to talk anymore tonight anyway. He was not only physically exhausted from the trip, but now mentally exhausted as well. He had a lot of new information to process, and he knew that even though he was tired, he might not actually fall asleep for a while.

Sam sensed that they were done outside for the night and trotted across the well-worn path leading through the grass and up to the steps. She didn't stop until she reached the back door, where she sat down and waited for Jack and Ben to catch up. When they entered the house, the kids were still in the front room, but they were talking more quietly than before and with much less enthusiasm. The house was darker now that the sun had completely set, and Ben was tempted to turn the lantern up but decided against it.

Gunner was no longer sleeping in the kitchen and had moved to the living room to be near the kids. The front curtains had been pulled closed, and Ben was glad to see that Joel and Allie were still exercising good judgment and doing their best to stay inconspicuous from any possible threats outside. Thankfully, they were still being cautious when it came to their safety. Just because they had made it to Maryland didn't mean they could relax and let their guard down.

If anything, now they would need to be more vigilant with the addition of the younger kids, especially once they headed back out on the road. Having a second vehicle would pose its own unique set of challenges, but at least they had the radios to communicate.

Ben had given much consideration to who would be riding in what vehicle, but up until now, he wasn't sure if Jack would be part of that equation. With that question answered, he was pretty sure how it would work out. Ben wanted Bradley and Emma with him and also knew well enough that Joel would want to be with Allie. That put Ben with Sandy and the younger kids in the Blazer, most likely with Sam. There was no way Gunner would be happy unless he was with Joel and Allie.

Ben had reservations about Joel and Allie making the trip on their own in the Jeep for many reasons, but he had to put those feelings aside. Not only was there little choice in their travel arrangements, but he had no real reason to object to it. Any other suggestion would lead to an argument from Joel, and Ben wouldn't have a leg to stand on. Both Joel and Allie were capable, and it was time to have faith in their abilities. He decided to let it go; besides, he could focus on helping Bradley and Emma adjust to life on the road.

It didn't take long for everyone to make their way to bed after Grandpa Jack reminded them all that tomorrow would come early and that there was a lot to be accomplished before they left. Ben's heart was heavy about the situation with Jack, but in spite of that, he was looking forward to tomorrow. He saw it as a kind of new beginning for all of them. He could put the trip here behind them, or at least try, and plan a fresh start by setting up the trucks as well as they could for the journey home.

In light of the news Jack had just laid on him in the garage, the practical side of Ben couldn't ignore the fact that they were likely to inherit a large amount of gear and supplies tomorrow. He had no doubt that Jack would insist on them taking just about everything they could cram, stuff, or tie down in the vehicles. And seeing as how there would be six of them now and two large dogs, they could certainly use all Jack was willing to offer.

As Ben lay there in bed, he began to mentally pack the trucks in his mind, trying to think of the things Jack was most likely to give them. It was better to think about that than the other things they had talked about tonight.

Ben's eyes grew heavy as a slight breeze came in through the window, and he felt comfortable for the first time in a while. The bed was small, and sharing it with Joel wasn't ideal, but he wasn't going to complain. The mattress was soft and felt good on his weary back. He was too tired to think any more today.

· 4 ·

Morning came painfully early as Ben awoke to the sound of a distant rooster crowing. It might have been the boisterous fowl that woke him, but it was the smell of food and fresh-brewed coffee that lured him out of bed. Joel was already up and gone, but not by long, as evidenced by the lingering steam in the bathroom.

Jack must have had the generator running again. Ben hated to see the man use so many of his resources and worried about what might happen if the doctors were wrong. What if he lived for longer than they expected? What if he outlived his supplies? He would starve to death here all alone.

Ben took a deep breath. It was too early to get his head twisted up over all that, and he didn't want to start the day with hypotheticals. He needed coffee and he needed a shower. He'd only had a chance to get cleaned up a little bit last night before helping Jack with dinner. Ben flipped the switch in the bathroom and the light flickered for a second before staying on. No point in running the generator for nothing.

Ben could have stood under the soothing hot water all day. The bed was plenty comfortable, but his back and left shoulder were still tight from days behind the wheel. Regardless, he kept the shower short and forced himself to turn it off after only a couple of minutes. They had a lot to do today and he wanted to get to it. He also wanted to take advantage of the cooler morning temperatures. He could already feel the humidity in the air and couldn't tell anymore if he was wet from the shower or if he'd started sweating already.

Ever since early June, when they left Colorado, the weather had increasingly grown hotter, or at least that was how it seemed. This wasn't the dry heat that he was used to; it was humid here, and at times, he felt like he could choke on it. All the more reason to get an early start.

As Ben stepped out of the bathroom, he found a neatly folded pile of clothes on the dresser. Sandy started a load of laundry last night while he was helping Jack, and someone must have finished it this morning. Ben picked up the newly dried T-shirt from off the stack of clothes and instinctively brought it to his face. He inhaled the fresh scent of whatever laundry detergent Jack used and felt the warmth of the shirt on his skin. It had been a long time since Ben smelled clean, and it felt like a luxury.

It was comforting to get dressed in clean clothes for a change, and he thought it was very fitting considering that today represented a fresh start for them all. Not just physically, but mentally as well. He had his kids now, and nothing that had happened on the way here mattered. At least that was what he told himself. They could put that all in the past and chalk it up to experience. The journey ahead of them was daunting—there was no denying that—but they were smarter now and they wouldn't make the same mistakes they made while traveling east.

Ben hastily pulled on his hiking boots as the smell of coffee and food continued to motivate him. He hesitated, but only for a second, as he reached for his 9mm on the nightstand. It felt unnecessary to wear it in the house, but he needed to set a precedent in front of the kids. He didn't want to alarm them or cause them to worry unnecessarily, but it was the reality in which they lived. The sooner they accepted this fact of life, the better.

He had to lead by example if he expected the others to carry a weapon and stay on their toes. There was no need to be lulled into a false sense of security just because they were at Grandpa Jack's house. Those were the types of mistakes he vowed not to make. If something happened, the nightstand might be too far away. There were no guarantees anymore, and they needed to be ready at all times.

As Ben descended the old wooden staircase, the creaks and groans gave him away, and Gunner and Sam were eagerly awaiting his arrival at the bottom.

"Hey, guys. What's going on this morning?" Ben gave each dog a quick scratch behind the ears. He was glad to see them getting along. He was a little concerned at first that there might be some rivalry between the two dogs, but nothing could be further from the truth as the two large animals bumped into each other playfully while leading the way to the kitchen.

"Good morning." Sandy was the first to look up from the table and greet Ben as he entered the room. Joel was seated across from her, and Jack was at the counter, pouring a cup of coffee that Ben hoped was for him.

"Still take it black?" Jack asked.

Ben nodded and took the mug. He sipped the piping-hot liquid and savored the moment.

"Help yourself. It's not much, but it's something." Jack motioned to an empty seat at the table, where there was one egg and a couple of venison sausage patties on a plate.

"The Smiths keep us stocked up on eggs in exchange for produce from the garden." Jack poured himself another cup of coffee, made his way back to the kitchen table, and sat down.

"Where are the kids and Allie?" Ben asked.

"Still sleeping. They were up late last night. They convinced Allie to play some board games before bed. I hung in there for a while, but I just couldn't do it," Joel said.

"Emma is glad to have another girl around," Jack added.

"Well I couldn't ask for a better role model for my daughter." Ben looked at Sandy.

Sandy smiled. "Thanks. She's always been mature beyond her years."

"I can't even begin to tell you what an asset she was to us on the trip out here. Both of you guys pulled your weight." Ben glanced at Joel as he ate. It didn't take long for Ben to devour the two links of deer sausage and single fried egg. He wished there was more, but it would do.

"Thanks for washing the clothes," Ben said.

Sandy shrugged. "Oh yeah, no problem. I wanted to finish last night, but I fell asleep waiting for the washer to finish. To be honest, it felt good to do laundry. It felt normal."

Ben understood what she meant. Things they had once taken for granted, like flipping on the light switch to illuminate a room or brushing your teeth with water from a running faucet, were luxuries now. These types of things were conveniences of a former life and were now only afforded to them on rare occasions.

With Ben's plate empty, Gunner and Sam reluctantly moved from their positions on either side of him, where they were anxiously waiting for a few scraps.

"Maybe you'll have better luck with the kids." Ben watched as the two dogs abandoned their begging tactics and started for the back door.

"I'll take 'em out," Joel offered.

When Joel got up from the table, Ben noticed the absence of his pistol.

"Forgetting something, aren't you?" Ben asked. Joel looked stumped for a second as he glanced around the room and then back at his dad. He shrugged. "What?"

"Your gun." Ben raised his brow.

"Okay." Joel sighed loudly and rolled his eyes.

"Hey, always carry. That is the rule we made. Remember? At least for now or until things change. You don't know what's outside that door!" Ben was irritated with Joel's response and body language, but that changed as he began to feel bad for raising his voice. Joel was still just a kid. It was hard to remember sometimes, but that was because he hadn't been able to act like a kid lately, but that wasn't Joel's fault.

"I know. Sorry." Joel slouched as he headed upstairs. Now Ben felt even worse about how he had reacted and even a little guilty for not letting his son be a kid for a change. He certainly deserved it, and he probably felt relaxed here at his grandfather's. But that was also the type of attitude that could get you in trouble.

"I just want you guys to be safe," Ben said, but Joel was already halfway up the stairs and out of sight. Gunner and Sam stood at the door, looking back at the room full of people and confused about what was going on.

"I'll let them out." Jack started to get up, but Joel's heavy footsteps came from the stairs already. He breezed through the kitchen and out the back door, only stopping long enough to wait for the dogs to follow him outside.

"We haven't had much trouble around here. He'll be all right," Jack tried to reassure Ben. And while Jack might have been right, it was good to stay in the habit of how they did things. Joel wouldn't always just be stepping outside at his grandfather's house.

"You might feel differently if you'd seen some of the things we have," Ben reasoned.

"It's true. I used to think people were inherently good, but I don't know anymore." Sandy took a sip of coffee and leaned back in her chair. Ben had to agree with her, although if he was being honest, he was always a little cautious when it came to trusting people until they proved they could be trusted. All that had happened over the last couple of weeks had only proven that to be a prudent viewpoint. Outside the small group they met in Cloverdale and a couple of others, Ben was disappointed in humanity as a whole.

· 5 ·

After breakfast, Ben helped Jack clean up in the kitchen while Sandy made the others who were still sleeping a plate of food and covered it with foil.

"We'll probably cut the generator off in a little while." Jack looked at his watch. "I'll let it run until eight if you want to let the kids know their chance to get a shower won't last long."

"Okay, I'll let them all know," Sandy said.

"Ben, how 'bout giving me a hand with this ice?" Jack handed Ben the bucket while he held onto the counter for support. Ben was made aware once again just how much Jack had aged as he stood next to him in the kitchen. Jack was always a little shorter, but now, Ben seemed to tower over him by a good six inches or more.

Sandy headed upstairs to wake the rest of the kids while Ben and Jack headed outside. As soon as Ben stepped out onto the sun-bleached deck, he was reminded of how quickly it was going to get hot, and his sense of urgency was renewed. Joel was standing in the shade of a large oak tree, throwing and old retrieving dummy to Gunner and Sam.

"Don't work 'em too hard. It's hot out here," Jack called out to Joel.

"I won't. I'll give them some water when they're done," Joel answered without looking away from what he was doing.

Jack opened up the outbuilding and led Ben inside and back to the cooler.

"I wish I could send you guys with more of this venison, but it won't keep without ice. Well, at least you can take enough with you to have dinner the first night on the road." Jack was half-talking to himself as he pushed a few things around in the cooler. "I talked to Joel about me staying here in case his mother returns. I didn't want you to have to lie to your son. You can tell him the truth someday when the time is right," Jack said before stepping aside to let Ben dump the bucket.

Ben nodded and remained silent, but inside, he wrestled with the urge to bring up the subject of Jack going with them again. He needed to make peace with Jack's wishes, something that was easier said than done. Otherwise, they could spend the whole day arguing their cases to one another, and Ben knew that, in the end, Jack wasn't going to change his mind. So rather than waste what was possibly the last day he would ever spend with the man by debating what was right, Ben decided to let it go and focus his efforts on gearing up the trucks.

They opened the two large overhead vehicle bay doors to let in the light and a little air. Ben pulled the Blazer out into the sun and made room inside the outbuilding to set up a staging area where they could sort through the gear. He had a rough idea of how he wanted to repack the Blazer, but he wasn't sure what they were going to end up with after they went through Jack's stuff.

Given Jack's current situation, Ben figured that he would offer them just about everything he had. And while they could use whatever supplies he was willing to give them, there was a limit to what they could reasonably carry. The Blazer was already loaded down pretty well. Ben could make some room by moving a few things around and organizing what they had, but there was no getting around the fact that he still had to squeeze four people and a large dog in there. The trip would be tough enough, and on top of everything else, there was no need to make it uncomfortable.

Ben also knew that, realistically, the Jeep wouldn't carry that much gear, either. He was thankful that Jack had put the time and money into fixing it up, but it wasn't a large vehicle. There was no back seat in the Jeep Scrambler; as far as Ben was aware, there never had been, so it was basically a small pickup by design. It was fortunate that it had the rare full soft top that covered the entire back end, unlike most Scramblers, which sported the standard half top only. Of course, it was a soft top and wouldn't provide any real protection from anything other than the elements.

That also meant there would be no way to really lock the Jeep up and secure things inside. Jack had installed a large lockable box in the rear of the Jeep where the back seat would normally sit, but Ben decided to remove that and make room for supplies and one of the dogs.

He imagined Gunner would ride with Joel and Allie. Over the course of the trip here, the dog had become very attached to Allie, not to mention that Gunner was Joel's dog, after all. It was probably for the best, as Bradley and Emma were close with Sam, and Ben thought that having a little piece of their former lives here would be good for them. He hadn't planned on adding another large dog to the mix—or any dog for that matter. But maybe having Sam along would provide some comfort for his younger kids.

As Ben started removing the homemade lockbox from the cargo area of the Jeep, he thought about another thing that was on his mind. Jack had put a lot of new components on the Jeep, including a new engine, and in his experience, there were always a few bugs to work out with a complete rebuild or replacement. Sometimes the problem or problems took a while to show up.

With just over a thousand miles on the remanufactured engine, it was far from proven, and Ben was well aware that some break-in issues would be likely. It would be trial by fire for the Jeep. The cross-country trek they were about to embark on would cover just over two thousand miles and include some major elevation changes at the beginning of the journey and then again at the end. The temperatures alone were enough to test any vehicle's cooling system, let alone that of an almost forty-year-old Jeep. They would have to carry extra water if they could find a place to stow it. Other than that, there was nothing else he could do to better prepare the Jeep for the journey. Ben knew that worrying was pointless, but it didn't stop him from doing just that.

By the time Ben had the storage box unbolted from the Jeep's bed, Joel had joined them in the garage and was ready to help his dad. Ben was glad to see Joel because the thick plywood box was too heavy and awkward for one person to carry on his own, and he wasn't about to let Jack help him.

With the Jeep ready to receive whatever could be squeezed in, they turned their attention to the shelves that lined the outbuilding's walls. The sturdy wooden shelves that Jack had built himself many years ago ran five shelves high and extended all the way up to the twelve-foot-high ceiling. The number of tools and the amount of hardware Jack had stored in here was something that was only possible by a lifetime of acquiring things.

Ben wished he had a truck large enough to take it all. Leaving this all behind was such a waste, but they had to be reasonable and pack only what they needed to survive. There was no point in even looking through the tools—or anything else for that matter—except the hunting and camping gear.

He had briefly considered the possibility of hooking Jack's aluminum John boat to the Blazer and using it like a trailer. The boat was lightweight, and if he took the small outboard off, it would be even lighter. But Ben remembered some of the situations they found themselves in on the way here, and the thought of adding a boat to the mix quickly lost its appeal. Besides, by the time they finished loading the boat with extra stuff, it wouldn't be lightweight anymore. It was better to travel with only what they needed and have the ability to pull over and disappear into the woods if the situation warranted—something that would be extremely difficult with an eighteen-foot boat in tow.

Jack instructed Joel to set up a step ladder so they could reach the top shelves and begin sorting through the dust-covered supplies. Sam found a spot on the cooler concrete floor nearby; exhausted, she lay sprawled out and remained motionless, other than for her heavy panting. Gunner did the same after he helped himself to the bucket of water Joel had set out for them.

The temperature was a little cooler in the shade of the building, but with the added humidity, it was still oppressive. Ben was amazed that everything around them was so dry when it was this humid. Maybe the atmosphere was changing; maybe they would see some rain soon.

Jack had an old-fashioned mercury thermometer mounted on the wall, and Ben had to give it a second look to make sure he was seeing it right. It was already reading an impossible ninety-four degrees. Ben wasn't that familiar with average summer temperatures for June in Maryland, but he didn't think that was right.

Jack noticed him studying the thermometer. "Yeah, it's much hotter than it should be."

"It's pretty brutal, and we're not even in the sun." Joel wiped his brow with an old shop towel. "Maybe I shouldn't have played with the dogs so hard," he added.

"They'll be all right. It's us I'm worried about." Ben looked at his watch. It was just after eight in the morning, and it was almost unbearable out. At this rate, they weren't going to last long out here, and if the temperature rose too much, they might reach a point where they would have to quit until the evening.

It was disappointing for Ben to think they might not get it all done in one day. He was hoping to finish loading the trucks today, with the exception of a few last-minute things, and have a down day tomorrow here at the house. They could all use a break after what they had been through, even if it was just a short intermission from their chaos-filled lives. They had plenty of unknown challenges approaching in the near future, and those were just the things they could plan for. Who knew what other unforeseen problems they would run into on the way back? There were sure to be some.

Ben wasn't naïve enough to think that it would be smooth sailing all the way to Colorado. There were twice as many of them now, and that meant twice the responsibility. He felt the pressure building, and its weight on his conscience was very real.

· 6 ·

They worked at a slow but steady pace for a while, making sure to stop and drink water every so often, but they were fighting a losing battle against the ever-rising temperature and eventually reached a point of exhaustion. It was almost noon, and the sun blazed down on them with full force now. Even in the shade of the outbuilding, the heat was stifling.

It didn't seem to bother Jack that much, though. In fact, he seemed to come to life a little as they pulled down the hunting gear. He moved aside dusty bags of Teal and Mallard decoys as they sorted through it all. It was the most life Ben had seen in Jack since they'd arrived. Jack paused for a minute and stepped back to look at it all as it lay spread out on the concrete.

"Lots of memories here," he said longingly. Ben recognized the windup; he'd seen it many times before and knew immediately they were in for a story or two. Jack loved to talk about his adventures and past hunting trips. Most of the tales revolved around duck hunting in his youth and the many times he'd been lucky enough to make it back with his life. "Hunting the bay in the winter can be dangerous business," he always said.

Of course, he could never leave out the time he'd almost drown and then nearly froze to death by falling into the marsh while hunting out of duck blind number 10 at Assateague Island National Park. He was after a decoy that had broken loose from its rigging due to the ice flow and was being carried out into the bay. Jack foolishly went after the decoy only to step into an unseen drop-off in the tea-colored water. He went completely under, filling his chest waders with freezing-cold water, and barely managed to make it back to shore. Soaking wet and hypothermic, he was forced to make the three-mile hike back to the truck in thirty-degree weather.

Jack told of some other close calls and included some more pleasant stories as well. Ben had heard most of them more than once, and so had Joel, but neither of them stopped him.

"It might be time to call it until the heat breaks," Ben suggested.

"Yeah, I think you're right," Jack agreed. His clothes were soaked through with sweat like Ben's and Joel's, even though he had mostly stuck to supervising and talking. Ben had watched the temperature slowly creep up to just shy of the hundred-degree mark over the last couple of hours. He'd been to some pretty miserable places while in the Army, but this rivaled the worst of them as far as the heat was concerned. The occasional smell of death that drifted into the building from the thousands of rotting chickens on the next farm over didn't add to the experience, either.

Jack abruptly turned away and headed over to the generator, where he wasted no time in turning it on. Ben wondered why he was running it now until he saw him head over to a large wall-mounted fan. The oversized commercial fan hummed to life as the blades reached their maximum speed and a strong breeze began to clear the stale, hot air out of the workshop. Joel moved closer to the fan and struggled to peel off his wet shirt as he basked in the fresh air. "That feels good," he said with a sigh.

To take advantage of the fan, Ben repositioned himself as well, then grabbed onto a support column to keep his balance as he closed his eyes and enjoyed the coolness. He was feeling a little dizzy now that he had stopped moving and was suddenly aware of just how much the heat was affecting him. It was a good thing they were quitting now. He'd had about all he could take for the time being. His thoughts were interrupted by the sound of Jack rummaging through the ice in the cooler. Ben opened his eyes to see Jack bent over at the waist and rummaging through the freezer. He finally emerged holding two ice-cold beers.

"I've been saving these." Jack held the bottles up in one hand. He handed one of the beers to Ben and the other one, to Ben's surprise, to Joel.

"I want some of that too, young man." Jack smiled while making eye contact with Ben as if he was trying to get his blessing in sharing the beer with Joel. Ben wasn't crazy about the idea and had never let Joel have a drink before, but considering the circumstances, he didn't see any harm in it right now. After all, this was the last time Joel would be with his grandfather. This was the last any of them would see of him. Ben pondered the magnitude of the moment as he rolled the cold glass bottle in his hand; it was already sweating enough to cause condensation to run down his hand.

Jack returned from his workbench with a plastic cup and held it out for Joel to fill.

"To a safe trip home." Jack held up the freshly filled cup before taking a drink. The way Ben was feeling, beer wasn't the best choice right now, but he reminded himself that this was for Jack's benefit and not his. It had been a long time since Ben had a cold beer, and the ice-cold liquid was refreshing in spite of his concerns. Ben glanced at Joel as he took a sip and then made a face.

"It's not bad," Joel remarked as he took another small sip.

"Don't get used to it," Ben added.

Joel rolled his eyes. "I know."

As much as Ben tried, it was getting harder and harder to see Joel as just a kid anymore. He hated to admit it, but his son was quickly transforming into an adult whether he was ready for it or not. Ben was worried about letting Joel have half a beer, and he had to admit it felt like a silly thing to worry about considering all they had seen and been through in the last couple of weeks. They stood around in silence for the next few minutes as they finished their drinks and surveyed what they had accomplished.

They had made pretty good progress despite the conditions, and the Jeep was beginning to take shape. They had to pack smart, though. The soft canvas top on the Jeep prevented them from carrying anything on the roof. Fortunately, Jack had a rear cargo carrier that mounted to the hitch-style bumper on the Jeep. On the rear carrier they could put the larger, bulkier items like Jack's spare five-gallon gas cans, similar to the ones they carried on the Blazer. Joel also found a couple of five-gallon plastic water containers that could ride back there as well. This left room on the inside of the Jeep for things that couldn't get wet or shouldn't be exposed to the elements. And thanks to Jack's generosity, there was plenty of that stuff to pack.

Jack had insisted that they take both full cases of MREs, leaving him with only the contents of the freezer and whatever vegetables he could wrangle from the garden. He made them promise to take his large supply of deer jerky, which was vacuum-packed in one-gallon bags. Of all the things Jack gave them, Ben was most grateful for the jerky. It would keep well, probably last them until they reached Colorado if they rationed it, and provide a much-needed source of protein on the road, not to mention that it would help break up the monotony of the freeze-dried and dehydrated meals that had become the staples of their diet. A few pieces of jerky thrown in with the rice while it cooked would go a long way toward boosting morale and their energy.

Jack felt bad that they couldn't take more from the chest freezer, but in this heat, it would be a wasted effort to pack more than a day's worth of frozen venison. On the morning of their departure, they would take a small amount of the meat with them in one of Jack's old coolers. But even packed in ice, in this heat, the top layer would be thawed and ready to cook by the time they found a place to camp on the first night.

They were also careful to leave an easily accessible spot open for Gunner to ride close to Joel and Allie behind the seats. The Jeep sat pretty high off the ground with its thirty-five-inch tires and modified suspension; there was no need to make it any harder for Gunner to load up into the vehicle than it already was.

The best way in for the sometimes-nimble dog was up and over one of the two front seats rather than through the small tailgate, thanks to the swing-away tire attached to the bumper. The full-size spare and rim weighed a fair amount, and the whole setup took a good deal of effort to operate. Besides, with the hitch-mounted cargo carrier loaded with water and fuel containers, it was no simple task to access the Jeep through the back. That also allowed them to pack the truck tight with gear all the way into the back and make it so Gunner wouldn't have to climb over everything to get in.

The Jeep had aftermarket seats that sat up off the floor, and there were big open spaces underneath, which were perfect for packing with odds and ends. Ben found an old holster of Jack's that fit Joel's 9mm and zip-tied it to the underside of the driver's seat. It would be a more comfortable place to keep the gun while Joel drove and would ensure that it remained easily accessible. The locking console between the seats also had a good amount of storage potential while leaving plenty of room on either side for Joel's AR and Allie's shotgun.

They also decided to put together a second roadside toolkit just in case. Ben hated to think about it, but if they were somehow separated, it would be a good idea for Joel to have his own tools. For that matter, he intended to fit the Jeep out so it had everything Joel and Allie needed to survive on their own. Of course, Ben would take a bullet before he willingly separated the group, but it didn't hurt to plan for the worst. He had no intention of letting them out of his sight for a second, but he knew all too well that things didn't always go as expected.

· 7 ·

Ben pulled the Blazer back into the outbuilding for the afternoon. They could resume outfitting the vehicles later, when the temperature returned to something more reasonable. As he backed the truck into its spot, he noticed how much room they had made just by transferring Joel's and Allie's things over to the Jeep. Maybe they wouldn't be as tight on space as he originally thought.

Joel closed the big overhead door once the Blazer was inside and proceeded to help Jack lock the place up while Ben gathered a few things they were taking inside with them to sort through later.

"Let the generator run for a little while. I want to make a little extra ice to pack the cooler for your trip," Jack said. With the outbuilding secured, they made their way across the dead grass to the house. Anxious to get out of the sun, they moved as quickly as they could, but not too fast—for Jack's sake. Even the dogs moved slowly as they laboriously climbed the steps to the house. Panting heavily, they reached the door first and stood with their heads down, waiting to be let inside.

The little bit of spark Ben saw in Jack earlier was gone, and he reluctantly accepted Ben's help to navigate the last couple of steps to the porch. Ben felt Joel's watchful eye as Jack struggled the rest of the way across the deck to the house.

Joel had to know there was more to the story, right? He was a smart kid, and Ben didn't believe for one minute that Joel was completely buying Jack's excuse for not coming with them. The younger kids, sure, but after the trip here there was no doubt Joel understood the odds of his mother making it back here were slim. But what could Ben do about it?

Ben expected the house to be stuffy and hot but was pleasantly surprised when he stepped into the dark, cool kitchen. A side benefit of leaving the generator on was that the house's air-conditioning unit was running. The thermostat said eighty-two degrees, but it felt ice-cold compared to the sauna-like conditions they endured outside.

"Oh man, that feels good." Joel stopped under one of the ceiling vents and let the cool air wash over him. They could hear Allie talking in the other room, but as they rounded the corner, Ben couldn't see anybody. The curtains were pulled closed to keep the sun at bay, and Ben's eyes took a second to adjust.

"You guys look worn out," Sandy said.

"Thanks for turning the generator on. I hope you don't mind. I have the icemaker going," Allie added.

"No, not at all. That's why I have it running, actually." Jack leaned against the wall.

"What are you guys doing?" Joel asked.

"Packing for the trip," Emma said. Ben's eyes had now fully adjusted, so he glanced at the various piles of stuff scattered around the room. He hoped they weren't trying to take all this with them.

"We're trying to get it down to just these two bags." Emma looked at Allie. "Right?"

"That's right, Em. We're getting there." Allie smiled. Ben was surprised by Emma's response to the nickname. She'd never really cared for the nickname that he was aware of, but she seemed happy about it now, judging by the smile on her face.

"You look hot, Dad. You too, Joel." Bradley walked over and felt his dad's shirt.

"It's really bad out right now," Joel answered.

"That's why we're taking a break until it cools down, buddy. We got a lot accomplished, though," Ben added.

"Yeah, we did pretty good considering I did all the heavy lifting." Jack laughed but let go of the wall as it turned into a deep cough and he nearly doubled over. He started down the hallway to the bedroom before he had fully recovered. Sam got up from her dog bed when she heard Jack coughing and approached her owner. Sam wasn't the only one who was worried; everyone went silent, afraid to address Jack's health.

"I don't know about you guys, but I'm ready for a cool shower and a nap. Make yourselves at home." Jack paused at his bedroom door at the end of the hall and turned to look at Ben." Do me a favor and turn that generator off in a couple hours, will you? The keys to the outbuilding are hanging by the back door."

Ben nodded. "Sure thing, Jack. Get some rest. We've got it covered." Ben was worried about Jack, but he didn't want to show his concern, afraid the kids would press him for information. If they found out the real reason Jack was staying behind, Ben wasn't sure how they would take it. Maybe if they knew the truth, it would force Jack's hand and he would have no choice but to come with them to Colorado. The kids would surely insist that he join them on the trip, knowing what fate awaited him here, alone. Jack wouldn't be able to say no to them, or would he? But it didn't matter. It wasn't Ben's place to tell them, and it would be going against Jack's wishes.

"I think I'm going to get cleaned up, too," Joel said.

"Yeah, that's a good idea, as long as the generator's running," Ben agreed. He'd grab a shower when Joel was done. No point in passing up the opportunity while they had it. There was no telling when they'd have these luxuries again once they left Jack's.

Joel headed upstairs and Ben took a seat in Jack's big leather recliner. It felt good to sit in the big, overstuffed chair and take a load off his weary feet. He wished he wasn't all sweaty, but to be honest, it felt so good to relax for a minute that he didn't care. He slipped his boots off as he watched Emma and Allie resume their attempt to organize Emma's bag. It did his heart good to see them sitting close to one another, and he could tell the two were bonding.

Ben wasn't worried about Bradley so much. He had a big brother to look up to, but he had never been more grateful for Allie than he was right now. Sandy was a welcome addition, too; although she was no replacement for the kids' mother, it was good to have her here nonetheless. Sandy seemed more than happy to chip in and help out wherever she could, but that made sense, based on Allie's personality alone.

Ben caught himself dozing off, and he fought the urge to sleep. He wanted to clean up and make sure he turned off the generator like Jack had asked, but he was afraid that if he gave in and slept, he might not wake up until much later. There was still a lot to do tonight, and as nice as it was to stay at Jack's and regroup, they were only putting off the inevitable. Maybe they should try and get on the road tomorrow after all.

The possibility of leaving tomorrow afternoon and driving during part of the night when it was cooler was appealing and would be easier on the trucks. But Ben decided against that when he thought back to John and Christine, the couple on their way to the Air Force base in Glendale, Arizona. They were trying to avoid the heat of the day, and where did that get them? The couple and their daughter were lucky to escape a near-collision with nothing worse than a bent tie rod. For a moment, Ben wondered what had become of them and if they ever found their son. Had they even made it to Arizona?

The risk wasn't worth it. They needed to stick to the plan and travel during the day. It was hard enough to make out highway signs as it was. With the way the weeds and tall grasses were growing along the roads, it wasn't going to get any easier as time progressed. They were just going to have to take their time and go easy on the trucks when they could, although that worked better in theory than in reality. Once they were on the road and underway, the inclination to push themselves and the vehicles in an effort to get home as fast as possible would be hard to resist.

On the way east, Ben worried often about the Blazer and counted himself lucky to have only suffered a minor setback with the alternator. A second vehicle was necessary but doubled their chances of a mechanical problem. They certainly couldn't count on finding another Vince or another town as friendly as Cloverdale the next time something like that happened. The hospitality extended to Ben and the others there was, unfortunately, the exception in the world they lived in now.

· 8 ·

"Dad... Dad. Joel is out of the shower if you want to get one, and Allie and her mom are making lunch." Despite his best efforts to stay awake, Ben had drifted off to sleep in the big recliner.

"Are you hungry?" Bradley shook his shoulder again.

"Oh yeah, thanks. I didn't mean to fall asleep." Ben glanced at his watch and saw that, thankfully, he hadn't been out long, although he felt like he could have used the rest. He heard Joel heading down the stairs, and the thought of having a shower and changing his clothes was enough motivation to get him up and moving again.

"Has anyone checked in on Grandpa?" Ben asked.

"I went to get him for lunch, but he was fast asleep, so I let him be," Sandy answered from the kitchen. "Lunch is ready, by the way."

"Thanks, but I'm going to get cleaned up first. Just save me a little," Ben said.

"All yours." Joel breezed through the living room, and the fresh scent of soap filled the air, making Ben feel even dirtier. He hurried upstairs and took a quick shower. As refreshing as the cool water was, there was too much he wanted to accomplish to linger any longer than necessary. He also didn't want to let his guard down, and he felt like that was exactly what he was doing at the moment. The others weren't as vigilant at keeping an eye out for trouble, and while Jack was sleeping and he was upstairs, Ben felt a little uneasy. While someone would have to be crazy or desperate to try something in this heat, some of the people they encountered on their journey so far were a little of both.

Ben wasn't familiar with the town of Berlin, Maryland, or the people who lived around these parts, but he had no reason to believe it would be any different than the other places they'd seen. Jack had mentioned a few neighbors and friends who all seemed to have each other's best interests at heart, but Ben wasn't naïve enough to think that there weren't some people around with less-than-good intentions. And he couldn't help but feel like they were advertising the fact that they had supplies while the generator was running.

The house sat a little way off the road, but without a crop of tall corn as a buffer, Ben wondered if someone could hear the generator from the road. It was a nice convenience and the air-conditioning felt great, but he would feel better once it was turned off. Jack's willingness to splurge on resources for their benefit was kind and a little morbid considering what Ben knew. Nonetheless, it made him nervous.

Ben wandered over to the big double window in the bedroom as he finished putting on a fresh T-shirt. Parting the curtains at the center, he squinted as the light blasted him in the face. He immediately felt the heat through the glass while his eyes adjusted, and he scanned the road in both directions as far as he could see.

He no longer felt guilty for assuming the worst about people, and being a little paranoid was healthy these days. He closed the curtain tightly, cutting off the shaft of light that penetrated the dust-filled room. Tucking his pistol into the holster, he headed downstairs to eat but decided to secure the generator before he had lunch. All the kids were in the living room, engrossed in a card game, and only Emma bothered to look up and acknowledge him with a smile. Sandy was cleaning up in the kitchen and had just finished dumping a load of ice into the bucket.

"Feeling better?" she asked.

"Lots." Ben smiled as he grabbed the bucket. "I'll be right back in. I just want to turn the generator off and get this in the cooler." The sound of the door opening drew both dogs' attention, and within seconds, they were through the kitchen and out the door. He reached back in and grabbed the keys before closing the door and sealing the heat out of the house. It felt just as hot as it had before they quit gearing up the Jeep. The dogs were less enthusiastic now that they were outside, and they seemed to regret their decision to tag along as they lagged behind Ben through the brown grass.

Was it this hot in Durango? As thoughts of clear, running streams and high desert forests came to mind, Ben decided it likely wasn't. Oh how he missed the fresh air and open spaces of the Rocky Mountains. He felt claustrophobic here. He always had, even before all this, when he and Casey had visited Jack, and the oppressive heat and humidity only added to that feeling. Once they returned to Colorado, Ben might never leave again, if he had his way.

He unlocked the door and let the dogs in first. It wasn't cool inside the building, but it was out of the sun, and that was a relief. Sam found what was left of the water Joel had set out for them earlier, and she drank heavily while Gunner waited for his turn. Ben felt his way along the wall as his eyes adjusted once more to the darkness. He flipped the kill switch on the generator and thrust them all into a welcome silence.

He had no intention of staying outside any longer than necessary, and after he dumped the bucket of ice into the old chest freezer, he started for the door without wasting any time.

"Come on, guys," Ben called to the dogs. Sam was still drinking and Gunner, clearly disappointed that he didn't get his turn at the bowl, reluctantly turned to follow Ben. Sam looked up from the bowl, spilling water all over the floor where she stood staring at Ben.

"Come on, Sam. There's plenty of water inside." Sam finally started moving toward the door at an impossibly slow speed while Ben impatiently waited for the dog to exit so he could lock the door again. Sam was a good-mannered dog and had a few years on Gunner. She was beginning to show her age with a bit of white hair coming in under her chin, and Ben doubted the big dog's ability or willingness to jump into the Blazer on her own. He envisioned himself lifting Sam inside every time they stopped. Ben hoped Sam was up for the trip to Colorado—for the kids' sake, if nothing else. Bradley and Emma were both very fond of the dog, and Sam usually slept in Emma's bed when they stayed with their grandfather.

Ben barely reached the top of the steps when he heard something that made him freeze in his tracks. The unmistakable sound of a vehicle coming down the road caught his attention, and he raced across the last couple of feet of the deck to let the dogs inside. He wasn't sure who was coming, but he didn't want the dogs running out to investigate. Sandy was still in the kitchen, and as he made eye contact with her, she immediately sensed something was wrong.

"What's going on?" she asked.

"There's a car coming. Probably nothing, but keep everyone inside for now. I'll check it out." Ben closed the door before she could answer. He was anxious to get back outside and see who was approaching. He crossed the deck and swiftly made his way down the steps as the exhaust note grew louder. Taking a position at the corner of the house, he peered around the edge until he could see the road. Sweat built up on his brow as he waited and baked in the sun.

The approaching vehicle wasn't moving very fast. Why would anyone be out and about right now if they didn't have to be? Ben could think of a few reasons, and none of them were good. It was hard to tell which direction the vehicle was coming from, and the flat landscape made it impossible to get a better vantage point. He hated feeling helpless, but all he could do was wait.

He finally caught a glint of sunlight off a windshield as the truck came into view. It was an old green and white Chevy pickup. Seeing an old truck wasn't anything new, but this one looked to be from the 1950s, if he had to guess, and it was in great shape. Someone had restored the classic Chevy and put some serious time into making it look new. Ben couldn't help but notice the shiny paint and bright chrome wheels glistening in the sun. The truck was nice to look at, but he was disappointed to see it slow down near the end of the gravel lane that led to Jack's house.

Ben jumped a little when the door to the house slammed shut, and he spun around, ready to tell whoever it was to get back inside, but he bit his tongue when he saw Jack. Ben turned his attention toward the road while Jack made his way down the steps and over to where he was.

The Chevy was close now, and Ben could see its occupants. There were two men in the truck, and they were eyeballing Jack's place pretty heavily. He really wished he had his rifle handy so he could get a better look at them. His gut told him they were up to no good, and he immediately wondered if they had heard the generator.

Ben felt Jack's hand on his shoulder. Using Ben for support, Jack leaned around the corner to get a look for himself. The Chevy slowed down even more as it crept past the end of the driveway; its occupants were still looking the place over. What did they want? Were they friends of Jack's?

"You know them?" Ben asked.

"I know the truck, but I don't know who's driving it." Jack shook his head. "That ain't the Hudsons."

Ben hated that his instincts were right. He'd known they were up to no good from the second he'd laid eyes on the two men in the truck. He wasn't sure what bothered him more: the fact that his mind worked that way or the fact that he was right.

If they weren't the owners of the truck, then Ben could assume the worst about them and their intentions. Thankfully, the Chevy kept moving, and Ben was relieved to hear the exhaust bark as the truck accelerated quickly and sped out of sight. Ben watched for a bit until he was sure they were gone, but Jack had stopped watching the vehicle a while ago and was standing upright behind Ben with a concerned look on his face.

"I hope Alan and his wife are okay," Jack said half out loud.

"Come on. Let's get back inside. Whoever they are, it looks like they have somewhere else to be, at least for now." The two made their way back inside, and even though the air-conditioning was off, Ben felt instant relief from the heat as he stepped into the kitchen. As his eyes adjusted to the dark interior of the house, he made out Sandy and the kids waiting in the kitchen.

"Who was that?" Joel asked.

Ben glanced at Jack, back at Joel, and then at the others, who were all gathered in the kitchen to hear the news.

"I don't know. Your grandpa recognized the truck, but someone else is driving it. They probably stole it from the owners, and who knows what else." Ben considered leaving out the last part but decided to tell it like it was. The others might as well know everything, even Bradley and Emma.

What good would it do to keep his suspicions about the truck and its occupants from them? Besides, a little fear was good; it kept you on your toes. And Ben wanted them to be alert. In his experience, bad things always happened when things seemed to be under control. He didn't consider himself to be a pessimist, but more of what he liked to call a realist. He was glad to see the kids playing games in the living room and enjoying some normal downtime, but reality was right outside that door, and it wasn't kind or forgiving of mistakes.

Ben looked at the kids and Sandy, who stood there in the kitchen in silence, no doubt thinking about what he had just said, and in that moment, it hit him. He was directly responsible for the welfare of all these people in front of him. Yes, Sandy was an adult and plenty capable, as were Joel and Allie, and they had proven that. But it was up to him to get them all home safe. He felt the weight of it, and the responsibility overwhelmed him for a second.

"Well, we'll just have to get packed up and get out of here as soon as we can." Joel stepped forward and put his hand on Ben's shoulder as if he could sense how his dad was feeling.

"But what about Grandpa?" Emma asked.

"Oh, you don't need to worry about me, Em. I'll be fine. I've got lots of friends around here. Besides, we don't know if the truck was stolen or maybe they were just borrowing it." Jack shot Ben a disapproving look.

Ben was getting tired of the lies, and he was tired of keeping the secret Jack had sworn him to keep. Normally, he'd be okay with leaving out details if he thought it would benefit the kids, especially the younger ones, but this was not one of those times. In fact, those times were long gone. It was a dangerous world out there, and it was full of dangerous people. The kids all needed to know that. It was unpleasant, but the sooner that type of thinking became the normal reaction to the unknown, like to the people in the truck, the safer they would all be.

· 9 ·

The kids made small talk among themselves as they found their way back to the living room while the adults stayed in the kitchen and talked.

"What time do you want to get back to work on the trucks tonight?" Sandy asked. "I can help if you let me know what needs to be done."

"Thanks. Maybe you and Allie can organize what's in the Blazer and come up with an inventory of what we have. That would be a big help," Ben said.

Sandy smiled. "It's the least I can do."

"Probably won't be cool enough until after dinner," Jack stated.

As much as Ben hated to admit it, Jack was right. He didn't like putting it off that long, but he knew that going back out into the heat wasn't smart. It wasn't cooling down anytime soon, and though he wanted to finish prepping the trucks, he also wanted to rest up for the trip ahead. It wouldn't do any good to exhaust themselves now and risk delaying their departure time. Since the people in the truck had checked the place out, Ben felt the urgency to leave now more than ever. They would be back eventually; it was only a matter of time.

As much as Ben tried not to, he worried about what would become of Jack after they left. The thought haunted him relentlessly. He felt helpless to do anything about it, but more than anything, he felt guilty. Ben kept reminding himself that Jack had made his decision and that all he needed to worry about was getting his kids, Allie, and her mother out of here safely. Ben also worried about the kids and their take on the whole thing. They would certainly be more worried now that some potentially dangerous people had paid them a visit.

Surely one of the kids would insist on Jack coming with them. Ben was surprised they hadn't pushed harder for his inclusion in the trip already. He figured that the only thing preventing them from asking was the possibility of their mother coming back to an empty house if Jack left as well. Little did they know that if Casey made it back, it would be a lost cause anyway.

Ben would be surprised if they made it out of here without the kids learning Jack's secret. In the short time they had been there, he'd noticed a major deterioration in Jack's health. Maybe it was the heat. Maybe it was the fact that he didn't have to fake it anymore now that Ben was here to take care of the kids. And in a way, Ben wished it was out in the open and the kids knew the truth, even if it meant temporarily adding a great deal of drama to their lives. At least it wouldn't be his burden to bear alone anymore.

Sandy's throat had been bothering her, and she finished making a cup of tea and excused herself to the living room so she could rest before dinner. Ben and Jack sat down at the table while they ate their now-cold lunch of rice and vegetables from Jack's garden. Ben was hungry, but the best part of the meal was the cold, refreshing sweet tea. They sat in silence as they ate their meals.

Jack broke the silence as he finished eating. "I've got some things in the bedroom I want you to have a look at when we're done eating."

Ben wasn't surprised by the statement; in fact, he had been waiting for Jack to say something like that. He knew Jack had a gun safe in his bedroom and a few nice weapons locked up inside. Ben hoped that he would offer them some of his guns and ammunition, but he wasn't about to ask. When it came to weapons and ammunition, they were in pretty good shape for the trip back, but adding a few quality pieces to their arsenal wouldn't hurt. Ben could always find a little extra room in one of the vehicles for those types of things.

They finished cleaning up from lunch and started for Jack's bedroom. On the way by the living room, Ben checked in on the others and saw that Joel and Bradley had fallen asleep on the couch. Sandy wasn't far behind in the recliner while Allie and Emma talked quietly. Seeing the girls talking warmed Ben's heart; in all the disorder and darkness that had consumed their lives, there was a little light.

Ben continued to follow Jack without interrupting the girls. Gunner and Sam were content to stay put as well, although Gunner's tail beat the side of the coffee table like a drum when he saw them, and Ben was afraid that it would wake everyone up.

"Stay," Ben whispered as he held out his hand, urging Gunner to stay put. Gunner put his head back down on the carpeted floor and quickly resumed his nap. As they entered Jack's room, Ben noticed the dresser top was littered with mostly empty prescription bottles and paperwork that must have been directions for all of it. There were at least a dozen little orange pill bottles scattered around. He wondered how long Jack had been out of his medications and if that was the reason his health was going downhill so fast.

As Ben predicted, Jack led him over to the safe, where he dialed in the combination like he had done it a thousand times before.

"Pull up the bench, will you?" Jack motioned to the bench seat near the foot of the bed. He struggled with the heavy safe door and then sat down with a sigh and remained quiet for a minute as he surveyed the contents of the gun safe. Ben stayed silent as well, not wanting to rush him or seem eager to take the man's guns. Whatever Jack decided to give them would be his only lasting legacy to the kids, and Ben realized the gravity of the situation. He sat back and gave Jack the time to do this how he wanted.

The first gun he pulled out wasn't what Ben expected, and he was surprised Jack owned anything like that. Jack handed the desert-tan Kel-Tec KSG 12-gauge over to Ben.

"I originally bought that for home defense, but to be honest, it's a little too much to handle for my taste." Jack didn't waste any time and began rooting around in the bottom of the safe for something else.

Ben hadn't ever had the chance to shoot a KSG, but he was familiar with it. He'd drooled over one at a gun show in Bayfield a while back but decided to be responsible and not spend the money. He knew why it was too much for Jack to handle, though, especially in his current state of health. The bullpup-style shotgun was only twenty-six inches long altogether and weighed just under seven pounds, if his memory served him correctly.

Jack slid a carton of double-aught buckshot out of the safe and slid it across the carpet toward Ben. "She'll take fourteen plus one of the two-and-three-quarter-inch shells."

"Thanks, Jack. This'll come in handy, I'm sure. I almost bought one of these a while back," Ben added.

"Good. So you're familiar with it?" Jack asked.

"Oh yeah." Ben nodded as he handled the weapon and toggled the magazine selector switch back and forth. The switch allowed the user to draw ammunition from two separate tubes that served as magazines and ran the length of the gun, feeding the main chamber. Each magazine could be loaded with a different type of shell, so you could have birdshot or buckshot loaded in one and slugs in the other. Each one held seven rounds of the two-and-three-quarter-inch shells, leaving room for one more in the chamber, which brought the total amount of ammunition available to the user up to fifteen rounds when the weapon was fully loaded.

It would be a welcome addition to their arsenal, and its size made it ideal to keep close at hand in the truck. The KSG wasn't meant for long-range shooting, though, and only sported a pair of Magpul flip-up sights, but it was easily lethal at fifty yards. The shotgun was set up the way Ben would have done it if he'd bought the one at the show. Manual flip-up Magpul sights were simple and always worked. They also allowed for an open field of view down the barrel. The tactical light mounted on the lower rail wasn't necessarily something Ben would have added, but it might prove handy, given their current situation.

Before Ben had time to fully appreciate the KSG, Jack handed him a smaller box of ammunition from the safe. Ben's eyes grew wide and he couldn't help but smile a little as he looked it over.

"Dragon's Breath?" Ben shook his head.

Jack smirked. "It's kind of a novelty, but it may prove useful down the road. You never know."

Dragon's Breath was a type of shotgun ammunition that Ben had only read about and seen used in a few videos. It was a flamethrower round filled with a magnesium-based incendiary metal compound. The flame would reach out over one hundred feet at four thousand degrees Fahrenheit, burning or melting just about anything in its path.

Jack pulled another rifle out of the safe before Ben had a chance to finish looking at the box, and he was less excited about this one. At first, it looked to be a basic AR-15 setup chambered in the standard .223 caliber. But then Ben noticed what was mounted on top, and his interest in the gun was reignited. It had a very nice 4 × 32 ACOG (advanced combat optical gunsight). The fixed magnification scope was a rugged combat-proven optic equally suited for CQB (close-quarters combat) or taking out a target up to eight hundred yards away, although Ben considered five hundred yards to be the practical limit of the scope with a .223-caliber weapon. The optic was also designed to be used in low-light conditions, with the tritium fiber optic-illuminated reticle making the best use of any available light. He was plenty familiar with the optic from his Army days and knew it was reliable.

"Here you go. Bought this one before Maryland went full communist." Jack laughed a little before it turned into a raspy cough.

"Nice." Ben smiled as he set the KSG on the bed behind him and took the rifle.

"Bradley and Emma can both load and shoot that without any help from me," Jack added.

"I appreciate you working with them on that, Jack." And Ben was. He regretted not being able to be there and teach the kids these types of things. The time they had on their visits to Durango was nowhere near enough for him to do a proper job when it came to firearms training and proficiency. That was something he believed should be practiced as often as possible. Ben held the AR up to his shoulder and looked through the scope. It was a welcome addition to what they already had. And as an added bonus, it was another gun that any one of the kids could handle.

But there was more to the AR than a nice optic. At first, Ben didn't recognize what Jack had pulled out of the safe, but eventually he realized what it was.

"Is that a suppressor?" Ben tried to hide the smile he felt creeping across his face.

"Sure is." Jack appeared proud of the little black tube in his hand.

Ben shrugged. "I didn't think you could get a permit in Maryland for that."

"You can't that I know of, at least not without filling out a mountain of paperwork. Nobody knows I have it. This little thing could get me in a lot of trouble. Well, it would have. I don't imagine it matters much anymore. I made it in the shop with a couple pieces of pipe and some steel wool. Works just like it should. You can't really hear much more than the bolt cycle when you fire the gun." Jack handed the suppressor over to Ben.

He looked it over and ran his fingers around the weld at both end caps. "What do you do with this?" Ben gave Jack a curious look.

"About half a mile that way through the woods"—Jack pointed—"there's these people that put out tons of cat food for all the feral cats around here. It got so bad that there were hardly any squirrels or rabbits around anymore thanks to the cats. They started getting bold and coming up to the house and the outbuilding. They were driving Sam nuts at all hours, and she got into a couple fights with some of the bigger ones that were brave enough to venture into the yard and challenge her. One of the neighbor's kids even had to endure a series of rabies shots thanks to the feral cats. I had to do something about it, so I started taking a few of them out. The problem was that they would all scatter at the first shot. So I made this little contraption, and well...let's just say we don't have a feral cat problem anymore."

Ben wasn't sure what to make of Jack's story, but he didn't blame the guy for taking action. The suppressor was well-made, and Jack had even taken the time to paint it black so it matched the AR-15.

Jack nodded at the tip of the rifle. "I've threaded the barrel and the pipe. They fit together perfectly."

Not only would this be a nice addition to their armory, but it was a game-changer as well. Ben thought back to more than a few scenarios during the way here and how this would have changed the outcome. Ben screwed the suppressor onto the end of the barrel and looked to see how well it fit together. Jack was right; it was a good, tight fit and sat below the field of view from the optic. Ben was impressed at Jack's handiwork, and it must have shown on his face.

"What? An old guy can't have a hobby? Besides, I get bored living here all alone." Jack smiled. For a moment, Ben forgot about all the bad things and it was just two guys talking about guns, but it didn't last for long, and Jack's expression turned solemn as he pulled out his custom Colt 1911 from the safe. The gun was special to Jack. Ben had only seen it a handful of times, yet he remembered it well.

Jack did a few tours in the Coast Guard in his younger days. When he and a small group of his shipmates were straight out of the academy, they had a few guns custom-made in honor of their duty assignment aboard a newly commissioned vessel. It was a beautiful piece, and the brushed nickel finish contrasted nicely against the mother-of-pearl grip inlays and gold Coast Guard emblem insert. He kept it in a thick leather holster with the words *Semper Paratus* embossed across the front. The pistol was older than Ben, but no one would ever guess that by the looks of it.

"I want Joel to have this." Jack didn't look away from the pistol. "If it's all right with you, that is."

Ben nodded. "Of course."

"Good, I'll give it to him in the morning before you leave. That is your plan, isn't it?"

"Yeah, if we can get everything squared away tonight. I'd like to leave early, before it gets too hot. With any luck, we can make it to the mountains before the heat of the day sets in or at least get as close as possible."

Jack shook his head and made eye contact with Ben. "Good, I don't know how much longer I can keep it together health-wise. I don't want the kids to see me get any worse."

Ben gave Jack a knowing look. "I understand."

"Well," Jack said abruptly and slapped his knee as he pushed himself up off the bench with a grunt. "The rest is just ammo, which you're welcome to, and some older hunting guns. Nothing more of any use to you probably, except maybe my deer rifle, but I'm giving that to my friend Bob Smith for taking care of my final requests after I pass. It's the least I can do to thank him for making sure I make it under the magnolia tree with Carol."

Ben was taken aback by Jack's casual attitude about his death and last wishes, but in a way, it was comforting to know that the man had made peace with his fate and seemed content in knowing it was his time. Ben tried to put himself in Jack's shoes, and for the first time, he started to understand Jack's logic. Other than not telling the kids, he got it. And the more he thought about it, the more Ben realized that if he were in the same position, he would likely do the same.

Jack was saving them the agony of watching him wither away and die. There was nothing any of them could do for him. Even if they could find the medicine he needed, it would only prolong the inevitable. Ben's attitude about the whole thing gradually shifted from frustration to appreciation, not only for what he was sparing them but also for the supplies; they would certainly prove useful during their trip home to Colorado. Then Ben realized that the guns and gear would be a tangible legacy for the kids to remember their grandfather by, but Jack's real legacy would be the help he gave them in his final days.

· 10 ·

Ben stayed in Jack's room for a little while as they talked about guns and hunting. The conversation made Ben forget about the world outside, at least for a little while. He was content to listen to Jack's stories while he organized the guns and ammunition into a neat pile for easy loading into the vehicles later. Ben tried his best to keep track of what Jack was giving him as he stacked it near the door.

Jack talked as he continued to unload the safe and hand things to Ben, only pausing to catch his breath occasionally or to fight off a coughing fit. He pulled out a box of cigars from the safe and opened it. Grabbing a handful for himself, he handed the remainder of the box to Ben.

"You might as well take these. I love 'em, but I can't even get through a whole one these days without coughing up a lung. I should have listened to Casey and quit a long time ago, but I guess that doesn't matter much now," he joked.

Ben didn't want the cigars but didn't want to offend Jack or hurt his feelings, either, so he took the box with a smile and a nod.

"Thanks, Jack." If they made it back to Cloverdale, maybe he'd pass them on to Vince. He wasn't sure if he smoked, but Vince struck him as the kind of guy who might enjoy a good cigar. Ben didn't know a good cigar from a bad one, but he was sure these were high-quality; Jack wouldn't buy anything less. Jack reminded him of Vince in more than a couple of ways. Stubborn and set in his ways but willing to give you the shirt off his back if he approved of you.

Ben could tell Jack was growing tired as the storytelling slowed and the breaks became more frequent. Jack seemed to be growing distant. Chewing on an unlit cigar in his mouth, he drifted off into a state of silence a few times as he stared at the safe. Ben was tempted to ask Jack if he was okay, but whenever he started to say something, Jack seemed to snap back into the present and pick up right where he'd left off.

Ben stepped back after he leaned the AR-15 and the Kel-Tecagainst next to the growing pile of ammunition cans. He'd been taking a rough mental inventory of the ammunition as he stacked it. By his calculations, they had added somewhere around three thousand rounds to their arsenal. Jack always bought in bulk and at wholesale places, and the result was a well-stocked safe. There were a few seven-hundred-round boxes for the .45, five hundred rounds of .308, which would come in handy for Joel's rifle, over fifteen hundred rounds of .223, and another tin with what must have been at least three or four hundred various 12-gauge loads, including double-aught buckshot and some duck load that probably wasn't intended for the Kel-Tec.

All in all, it was quite a haul and more than Ben thought they would end up with. It was definitely going to take up a bit of space in the trucks, but they'd figure out a way to get it in, even if it meant having to strap more gear to the roof of the Blazer.

Jack stood up from the bench and staggered a bit, catching himself on the safe.

"Jack, you okay?" Ben took a couple of steps toward Jack and prepared to help him stay upright.

"I'm fine." He held up one hand and waved Ben off while he used the other to hang onto the safe door. "I just got up too quick. That's all. I think I'm going to lie down for a bit while we wait for it to cool down." Jack made his way around to the side of the bed and sat down.

Ben didn't want to leave Jack alone just yet but felt like he was being pushed out of the room.

"You should get some rest, too, while you can. You've got a big day ahead of you tomorrow," Jack added as he lay back and put his feet up on the bed.

"Can I get you anything?" Ben asked.

"No, I'm good. Just close the door on the way out please."

What choice did he have but to leave? There wasn't really anything he could do to help anyway. Ben paused halfway out of the room and glanced at Jack before he pulled the door closed behind him. Jack's eyes were already shut as he lay still on the bed. The only thing Ben could hear was his labored and raspy breathing. He felt guilty for leaving Jack, and he couldn't help but feel like this was the last time he would see him. The idea crept over him like a dark cloud, and he shook it off. Jack was too stubborn to die yet. There was no way he wasn't going to see them off and say his goodbyes to the kids.

Ben tried to think about something else as he walked down the hall and approached the living room. With the loss of the air-conditioning, the house was starting to heat up now, and Ben thought maybe it was time to open some windows.

Everyone was fast asleep when he entered the living room. All was quiet except for the sound of Sam snoring loudly, with the occasional grunt thrown in for good measure. Ben tiptoed over the sleeping dogs and made his way across the room, toward the window. It might do them all some good to get some fresh air. In his opinion, there was nothing worse than waking up hot and sweaty, although that might be unavoidable.

But he decided against opening the window as he pulled back the curtain and was quickly reminded of just how bright and hot it was outside. Maybe it wasn't so bad in here. Ben squinted as he peered outside and scanned the road for any sign of the old Chevy from before, but it was empty and all was quiet. Maybe he should get some rest.

He didn't mind the idea of squeezing in a little more sleep. After all, they had real beds and a house where they could expect a certain amount of safety. Who knew where they would be sleeping tomorrow night? There was really nothing else for him to do right now anyway. But he didn't like the idea of everyone sleeping at once during the day. It was no different than at night, really, but it made him feel vulnerable nonetheless.

Somebody should stay awake and keep an eye out for trouble. At least that was what he thought as he sat down on the end of the couch near Bradley. Then again, Gunner and Sam would give them a heads up if somebody came snooping around. They were both good watchdogs, and Ben thought about all the times Gunner had launched into full-on attack mode over nothing more than a porcupine or a squirrel around the house. He certainly wouldn't stay quiet over a couple of strangers nosing around the place.

Ben tried to fight it at first, but when Bradley leaned over and settled in against his side, there was no denying the heaviness he felt in his eyes. The warmth of the room wasn't helping him stay awake, either, and before long, not even Sam's snoring could keep him awake any longer.

· 11 ·

Ben slowly opened his eyes as the sound of Gunner's low growl filled the room. He sat up, trying not to wake Bradley, who was fast asleep on him. He gently moved him off his side and back onto the couch. Ben rubbed his eyes while Gunner let out another low grumble, this time adding a small bark at the end while he began to get up. Sam was awake now, too, and joined in with a growl of her own. She rose off the floor surprisingly fast. Ben came to his senses while he watched Sam go to the front door and sniff the edges. Both dogs were fully awake now and clearly on edge about something. Ben doubted it was a squirrel.

The dogs' restlessness had woken everyone else now, too.

"What's going on?" Joel stretched as he stood up from the couch.

Sandy sat up in the recliner. "Is someone here?"

"I don't know." Ben made his way over to the window and moved the curtain out of the way just enough to see the road out front. He half-expected to spot the green Chevy, but there was nothing on the road or in the driveway. The dogs were still worked up, and it was only because of Allie and Emma's attempts to calm them that they refrained from launching into a full-blown fit of barking. Ben didn't see anyone outside, but the look in Gunner's eyes and the raised fur along his back told him otherwise. There were people here; Ben just couldn't see them yet.

Ben let the curtain fall back into place while he thought about what to do.

"I want you guys to stay inside and stay away from the windows. Joel and I will go check it out." Ben glanced at Joel. He looked surprised that his dad had included him in his plan for a change. Ben thought about going alone, but he wanted someone to watch his back. If it was the guys in the pickup, there would be at least two of them, but there was no way to know for sure.

The drive-by earlier was probably meant to check the place out. Maybe someone had seen them come in the other night or had heard the generator today. It didn't really matter, though; either way, they were going to have to deal with whoever it was.

Ben had to let Jack know what was going on. He hated to bother him or wake him up if he was sleeping, but he wanted someone with the kids. Jack was in a weakened condition, but he still had his wits about him, and he could still pull a trigger.

Ben swiftly maneuvered down the hall, toward Jack's room, careful not to make any more noise than necessary. It was an old house, and almost every step on the floorboards resulted in a squeak he was sure could be heard from outside. He hadn't really noticed it before, but it seemed extra loud at the moment. Not that it mattered much; whoever was out there already knew they were inside.

Ben looked back and signaled for Joel to stay put at the end of the hallway. Ben kept an eye on the windows as he passed the rooms off the hallway, searching for any signs of lurking shadows on the drawn curtains. He slowly let himself into Jack's room and crouched down by the bedside.

"Jack... Jack," Ben whispered as loud as he dared while he shook Jack's arm, but he remained motionless. Ben's heart began to race as he watched for any signs of life. He was about to check for a pulse when Jack startled to.

"What's happening? What's going on?" Jack coughed.

Ben jumped back but was relieved that Jack was still with them. "Whoa, easy. It's me, Jack. Somebody's snooping around outside."

"How do you know?" Jack asked.

"Well, I don't know for sure, but the dogs are worked up over something. I'm thinking those guys in the pickup are back."

"All right, I'm coming. Give me a second." Jack started to get up slowly.

"Joel and I can handle it. I just need you to keep an eye on things inside and keep everyone else calm and quiet." Ben hoped Jack wasn't offended, but he didn't have time to worry about that now. Besides, Jack was in no shape to do otherwise. Even he had to know that.

"Dad!" Joel whispered excitedly. Ben turned to look and saw Joel standing at the end of the hallway, waving him back out toward the kitchen.

"What is it?" Ben whispered back, not wanting to leave Jack's side until he was up and out of bed.

"I see someone out back by the garage. Hurry up." Joel spoke a little louder now, and the sound of urgency in his voice matched the look on his face. Jack was almost on his feet, and as Ben stood, he glanced over at the pile of ammunition and guns near the bedroom door. He thought about the possibility of there being more than one intruder and grabbed the Kel-Tec KSG along with one of the opened boxes of double-aught buckshot.

Ben stuffed the gun under his arm and began to load shells into the magazine as he started down the hall. He glanced back to make sure Jack was behind him and was glad to see him making his way out of the bedroom, his shotgun in hand.

"Go ahead, I got the kids," Jack said as he picked up speed and tried to catch up to Ben. Joel was still waiting at the end of the hall between the kitchen and the living room.

Joel pointed toward the kitchen window. "I saw a guy out back."

Ben was a little mad that he was looking out the window when he just asked them all to stay away from the windows, but he reminded himself that he had asked for Joel's help. Ben went to the window and peeked outside. Sure enough, there was someone there. The man door on the building had two small windows at the top of it, and a heavyset guy in a green hat was on his toes, trying his best to see inside Jack's outbuilding.

But that wasn't the most concerning thing. What really drew Ben's attention was the AR-15-style rifle he was holding. A person didn't bring a gun to snoop around someone's property with good intentions. Ben also noticed that the man was holding a small orange two-way radio. That immediately answered Ben's other question, although it didn't tell him how many others there were.

Jack had made it to the living room and was corralling the others up the stairs. Gunner willingly followed the kids, but Sam had to be told by Jack to "go." Sam reluctantly followed them up the steps with her tail tucked like she'd been caught doing something wrong. Once they were on their way, Jack joined Ben and Joel at the kitchen window. He leaned over and looked through the curtains himself.

"Don't recognize him," Jack said after a couple of seconds. "I'll keep everybody upstairs until I hear from you. Do what you need to do, Ben. Don't worry about us." Jack didn't wait for a response and headed for the stairs. Ben followed him toward the front of the house and nodded at Joel to follow. They couldn't very well go out the back with the guy there. Unless they used a window, there was only one other way out, and that was the front door. With any luck, whoever the guy in the hat was talking to on the radio wasn't out front.

Jack climbed the stairs to the halfway point, then turned around, sat down, and laid his shotgun across his lap. "I'll wait here." Sandy was at the top of the stairs with the kids, both of whom were wide-eyed and staring at Ben.

"Don't worry, guys. It'll be okay. We're just going to go see what they want and maybe try to scare them away."

"Come on, guys," Sandy said. "Your dad knows what he's doing. He and Joel will be fine." She coaxed the two away from the stairs and toward the back bedroom.

Ben nodded at them as they disappeared, leaving Sam alone at the top of the steps with her front paws hanging over. She growled once more, and Ben wondered if she had heard something else or if she was just unhappy about her place in all this.

"Stay put until I get out on the porch. I'll let you know when it's okay to come out. Once you're out, stay behind me a few feet and keep an eye out behind us." Ben turned away from Joel and crouched down by the door. He unlocked the deadbolt and slowly turned the worn brass knob. The door creaked open less than an inch as he peered outside. There was nobody on the porch, but using this door made him feel exposed. The other guy could be anywhere and most likely was watching the house while the other man took a closer look.

Ben pulled the door closed. He couldn't bring himself to step outside and into plain view without giving this more thought. Long ago, he'd learned to trust his instincts in situations like this, and they hadn't let him down yet. He and Joel would have to get outside some other way. Ben knew that as soon as he stepped outside the door, he would be an easy target. It would be a straight shot across any of the mostly open soybean fields surrounding them. He felt trapped in the house, and he hated the feeling.

· 12 ·

"What is it?" Joel asked.

"We can't go out that way. We'd be too exposed." Ben thought for a second, then looked at Jack.

"Does that window on the side of the house by the HVAC system work?" Ben knew some of the windows were tough to operate. The house was old, and despite the repairs Jack had made over the years, most of the original wooden windows were stiff at best, and some didn't open very far at all.

"It should work, at least enough to get out," Jack answered.

"All right. Come on." Ben nodded at Jack as he and Joel headed to the far side of the house. Ben didn't like Jack's answer about the window, but they were out of options. The other windows in the house would dump them out into the open or into the driveway, where there was no cover at all and they would be easily spotted.

The window they planned on using was in the laundry room on the south side of the house. It was the side of the house farthest away from the driveway and was separated from the adjacent field by only a small stretch of open yard. The window would allow them to drop down right behind the large outdoor HVAC unit. And while that wasn't really adequate cover, it was the best option and it sure beat stepping out onto the front porch in plain sight of any potential snipers.

Ben hated to think of things this way, but in his mind, that was what they were dealing with. Maybe he was wrong. Maybe he was overreacting, but he'd rather err on the side of caution than risk being shot at.

"Same thing as before. Let me get outside first, and then I'll let you know when it's okay to follow." Ben crouched by the window and slowly parted the curtain so he could access the sash locks. He tried the window, but it didn't move. He wondered when Jack had last opened it. He looked through the dirty glass and cobwebs to see if he could tell what was holding it closed. It looked like it had been painted shut. Joel shuffled to the other side and helped as the two tried to lift the stubborn window together. It began to move slowly, then finally broke free and slid up and over the top sash, fighting them the whole way.

The window opened with a squeak as the wood frame rubbed the inner sash, and Ben cringed as he heard the noise and sized up the next problem. The screen looked as old as the window and was rusted into place. It wouldn't budge when he pushed on it and he was forced to take out his pocketknife, but he paused as he was about to start prying at the edges. Why bother with all that? He plunged his Spyderco G-10 into the fiberglass screen and ran it around the metal frame swiftly. The blade slid through the screen with ease, and it fell outside in a crumpled pile under the window.

The house sat up on a concrete block foundation, with a crawl space underneath creating about a five-foot drop to the ground from the bottom of the window. Ben stuck his head out just far enough to get a quick glimpse in both directions before committing to the jump. Fortunately, the window was large enough that he could make the transition in one motion rather than having to crawl out.

When he landed behind the HVAC unit, his feet crunched in the dead grass and weeds. Ben glanced back up at Joel in the open window and held out his hand with his index finger extended, indicating for Joel to wait a bit. Ben stayed low and crept to the edge of the unit. He scanned the field directly in front of him and found himself wishing again that the farmer Jack leased the property to had grown corn instead of soybeans this year. He felt exposed but was grateful for the little bit of cover he had; it was more than he would have had on the porch.

The rows of dead, brown soybean plants were about eye level from his crouched position, and with a little effort, he could see over the tops and to the woods on the far side of the field. He scanned the edge of the wood line for any signs of movement but saw nothing. Satisfied that his immediate area was clear, he decided that it was time to move. He needed to deal with the known threat first, and that was the guy out back by the garage.

Ben's plan was to try and get close to the intruder, then observe and listen at first. Maybe he'd be able to eavesdrop on their conversation and be able to figure out where the other guy was. He didn't like the fact that there was one or more people out there and that he had no idea where they were hiding. But to do any of this, he had to get closer. Hopefully the guy was still there. Ben made his way to the edge of the recess where the HVAC equipment sat and motioned for Joel to drop down and join him on the ground. Ben was busy moving toward the edge of the house when he heard the grass crunch behind him. He turned back to see Joel and was glad that he had the Glock drawn and ready.

Ben made eye contact with his son and pointed past him, in the opposite direction he was headed, with two fingers. He wanted Joel to watch his back as he made his way to the corner and confirmed the man was still there. Joel understood what he meant and positioned himself so he had a good view of the road and the front of the property. Ben had used that signal many times before with Joel, but it had been when they were hunting elk or mule deer. That couldn't have been further from what they were up to today.

Today they were hunting a different type of animal altogether, one that preyed on the weak and unprepared. These people probably knew Jack lived here alone, and they might also know that he was in poor health. In fact, they were probably counting on it, and in Ben's eyes, that was even more despicable.

· 13 ·

Ben wasn't sure what pissed him off the most about what was going on: the fact that these two idiots, if it was the two guys in the Chevy, were trying to break into Jack's outbuilding and steal supplies or that they had ruined what could have been an otherwise peaceful afternoon and chance for all of them to catch up on some much-needed rest.

And once again, he was nearly soaked in sweat and covered in dirt and grass from slinking along the ground. It seemed that he found himself in this position more than any other these days, and he was getting tired of it. But even worse, it wouldn't be the last time they went through this or a situation like this.

Ben glanced back at Joel one more time before he reached the corner of the foundation, but Joel was looking the other way, as he had been asked. Ben refocused his efforts on being stealthy and went prone as he peered around the foundation. This wasn't going to be as easy as he thought. From here, he couldn't see the side door on the outbuilding. He would have to make his way over to the deck and get underneath it to establish a line of sight with the door and the last place he saw the would-be thief.

He moved back from the corner and got up to his knees while moving toward Joel.

"I need to get closer. Move here after I go," Ben whispered.

Joel nodded and followed him back to the corner. He double-checked the safety on the KSG to make sure it was off, then ran his thumb over the button just to be sure. He wasn't familiar with the nuances of the gun yet, and he wanted to make sure he was good to go. This time, he remained on his knees as he peeked around the corner and held the shotgun at the ready, scanning the yard over the end of the barrel.

Out of the corner of his eye, he saw Joel move into his spot as he started for the deck. Making sure to stay low and close to the foundation, he traversed the twenty-foot distance to the deck before stopping behind the wooden steps. A perimeter of lattice wrapped around the outside of the structure, but thankfully, it had fallen away in some locations, making it possible for Ben to take a position under the deck and in the shadows.

From this angle, he could clearly see the north side of the outbuilding. The man was still at the door, only now he wasn't trying to look through the windows and was instead working the door with a crowbar around the knob and deadbolt. Ben hadn't noticed the crowbar before now, but it clarified the reason they were here, not that there was ever any doubt.

The two-way radio was still clipped to the man's belt as he pried the door, and Ben wondered if he had missed a conversation or if the guy had just decided to go for it on his own. A piece of brick molding popped off the doorjamb, leaving a splintered mess near the door handle as the man cursed about his lack of progress.

Ben weighed his options and glanced back toward Joel. He couldn't see Joel now, either, which was a good thing. At least he was staying far enough behind the corner to remain hidden. He had to do something soon. The heavy-duty locks Jack had installed on the door were holding up pretty well, but they wouldn't last forever.

The man suddenly stopped working at the door and leaned his crowbar and rifle against the side of the building. He pulled up his T-shirt and wiped his face, exposing his large white belly. This guy wasn't hurting for food; Ben was sure of that. In fact, he was really out of shape and dirtier than Ben or the kids had ever been in the two weeks it took them to get here. And it was clear that his effort to gain entry to the building had pushed him to his physical limit.

The man let out a loud sigh and lumbered around to the front side of the building. In a shaded area, he leaned against the building while he continued to catch his breath for a moment. He was standing a good ten feet from where he had left his rifle and the crowbar.

Ben glanced back to the corner of the house where Joel was hiding. Thankfully, he was still out of sight and well around the corner. With any luck, Joel had seen the man move to the new position and had scooted away from the edge a little.

Ben calculated the distance between him and the guy, and his mind raced as he weighed the possibility of rushing him. If he could get out from under the deck without being seen and set himself up for a clear sprint, he figured he had a pretty good chance of reaching the guy before he could make it back to his weapon. The AR-style rifle the guy had was up with a large scope, so even if he managed to grab it in time, Ben would have the advantage, since aiming through the scope at that range was useless. Of course, the guy could get a lucky shot off from the hip. He would be shooting not only at Ben but at Joel as well if he fired in this direction.

And there was the other guy. The fat man wasn't carrying a two-way radio to talk to himself.

Ben had no idea where the other guy was hiding, but he was sure he wasn't far. He was probably somewhere just out of sight, waiting and watching for someone from the house to fight back.

Ben's body tensed up as he began to inch toward the opening in the lattice, but he froze when the man reached for his radio.

"I can't get in," the fat man said into the radio, breathing heavily.

"Have you tried the crowbar?" the radio crackled back.

"What do ya think I been doing?" he replied, even more frustrated now. He pushed himself away from the building and walked toward the door and his rifle. Ben watched as his chance to rush the man faded. But that was okay; if the other guy was forced to come help him, at least Ben could get a better idea of whom they were up against.

"We're gonna need the truck," the fat man said.

"Have you seen anybody around there?" the radio voice came back.

"No, nothin'. Just hurry up. I'm dying out here. It'll be worth it if there's a couple nice-looking old trucks in here that will probably run." The man leaned up on his tiptoes as he struggled to look through the small windows at the top of the door again.

"All right. Calm down. I'm on my way," the voice on the radio called out and then went silent.

The fat man muttered something under his breath and went back down to a normal standing position before he headed over to his previous spot in the shade. He was away from his gun again, and Ben thought about taking him out before the other guy arrived. If he knew how far away the fat man's help was, he probably would have, but he didn't want to lose the element of surprise and get caught in the open when the other guy came around.

And he was glad that he decided to stay put. Not more than a few seconds later, he heard the crunch of gravel and the familiar exhaust note of what sounded like the Chevy pickup. Sure enough, before long, the Chevy came around the corner of the house and pulled up in front of the outbuilding. A tall, thin man took his time climbing out of the truck as he cautiously looked toward the house and the surrounding area. He sported a pistol in a holster on his belt. Ben couldn't make out what type of gun it was, but he could tell it was a fairly modern-looking semiautomatic pistol. He also carried a large hunting knife in a sheath on his opposite hip.

"You sure there's nobody around?" the guy asked as he casually made his way over to where his friend was hiding from the sun.

"I haven't seen anybody. You got any water in there?" The heavyset man wiped the sweat from his face and started for the truck.

"Yeah, there's some on the front seat." The tall man ignored his sweat-soaked friend and continued toward the door of the outbuilding. "Don't drink it all," he added. No longer surveying the area, he focused his attention through the windows at the top of the door and peered into the garage.

"Maybe the old guy finally died," the fat man said between large gulps of water from an old jug.

"Probably. He hasn't been looking too good lately."

"Good, I don't like killin' people."

"Get over it," the thin man scolded. "That's just the way it is now. We wouldn't have that truck if we did things your way." He shot his friend a stern look. The fat man didn't respond and instead dropped his chin to his chest, clearly trying to avoid eye contact.

Ben wasn't surprised at the thinner man's comment, but it gave him chills just the same. It also confirmed his suspicions about the two, not that he needed confirmation, but it helped clear his conscience about taking action.

These two had been watching Jack's place and waiting for an opportunity to take advantage of him. He was relieved that the men hadn't seen him and the others arrive last night or when they were working outside earlier, but more than anything, he felt a sense of anger well up inside his chest.

These lowlifes had been watching and waiting for a chance to take what they wanted, and they were clearly willing to use any means necessary to get it.

Ben hated thinking about what would have happened if he hadn't arrived when they did. Emma and Bradley probably would've been forced to fend off these two on their own, given Jack's current state of health. He shuddered at the thought of it.

Emma and Bradley were fighters and wouldn't have made it easy for the thieves, but against two armed adults, the outcome would have been grim for his kids. Ben stared at the men in disgust as his imagination played out a couple gruesome scenarios.

"Grab the chain out of the back of the truck. We'll pull this door off the building." Letting himself down off the balls of his feet, the tall man backed away from the door and looked toward the truck.

"See, I told you. Lots of good stuff in there, right?"

Ben had seen enough, and he knew it was time to take action before these two pieces of trash went any further with their plans to break into the garage. But how would he do it? He thought about the fact that not only Joel, but Emma, Bradley, and the others as well, were all watching. He'd told them to stay away from the windows, but there was a good chance they were peeking out from behind a curtain at one of the rear-facing second-floor windows.

Joel and Allie were nearly eighteen and had already seen more than Ben wanted them to. Not that he had any choice in the matter. But Emma and Bradley were far too young to be exposed to this type of violence. It wasn't fair to them, and he hated everything about this moment and what he knew he had to do. The thought of his kids watching him kill someone made him sick to his stomach, but it didn't change the reality of the situation. Would life ever return to any type of normalcy, and if it did, would his kids be able to forget all they had seen and been through?

Ben knew the answer to that question as he bit down on his lip and prepared to make his move.

· 14 ·

As the two men laid out chain between the door to the outbuilding and the truck, Ben started to make his move. He was hiding behind a support post for the deck and the thick wood lattice that wrapped around the back part of the structure. The lattice prevented him from getting a good bead on either of the guys. Ben didn't want to take any chances.

He needed to do this quickly and accurately. There was no point in drawing this out any longer than he had to, and there was no point in trying to reason with these people, nor did he want to try. He flipped the magazine switch over to the slugs he had loaded on the left side of the KSG and moved quietly on his stomach toward the opening in the lattice. Just a few more feet and he'd be able to get on his feet and have a clear shot at the men.

BOOM.

Ben was startled by the gunshot, and he instinctively dropped back down to the dirt. Jack had taken a shot from one of the second-floor windows. So much for the element of surprise. When Ben looked up, the thinner guy was on the ground, and the big guy was frozen in his tracks halfway between the truck and the garage. The remaining intruder didn't stay still for long, though, and he started for his rifle, which was still leaning near the outbuilding door. But Ben still had a ways to go until he could get out from under the deck. Scrambling the last few feet, he emerged from his hiding spot and began to bring up the KSG and shoot.

Ben wasn't quite in position as the man reached his rifle and began to shoulder it. But Ben was out in the open now, and the man noticed him as he crawled out from under the deck. As soon as he saw Ben, he readjusted his stance and swung the rifle in Ben's direction. Ben's hiding spot had put him at a serious disadvantage, and Jack's shot had caught him off guard. He wasn't going to get the shotgun up in time to get a shot off. The only thing he could think of at that moment was his kids and the fact that they would have to make their way to Colorado without him.

BANG... BANG!

Ben tensed up and prepared for the pain of impact, but the bullets whizzed by him. He glanced down at himself for a second, then brought the shotgun up the rest of the way to fire on the man, but he didn't need to. The man hadn't fired the shots—Joel had.

The intruder was now holding his chest and had dropped the rifle. The bloodstain quickly grew out from under where he clutched at his shirt. Ben spun around to see Joel standing at the corner of the house, his Glock still pointed at the guy. Ben was shocked to see Joel standing there and noticed that his face was pale white; his wide-eyed gaze looked past his dad and remained fixed on the man he had just shot.

Turning back to face the intruders once more, Ben was just in time to see the first man, whom Jack had shot, somehow rising to his knees. Steadying himself on the ground with one hand, he had his pistol drawn and aimed at the second floor of the house with his other. Time seemed to move in slow motion for the next few moments, and Ben couldn't get a shot off quickly enough.

BANG.

The man squeezed off a shot before falling back onto his knees and holding his gut. Then he looked in Ben's direction and began to raise his pistol again. But it was no use. Ben already had a bead on him and was halfway through his trigger pull. The KSG gave a stout kick as the slug launched from the barrel and found its target.

The man jerked back as the slug tore into his chest and knocked him over. Knees still bent, he lay completely still in an unnatural position. Ben wasn't taking any chances and sprinted to the bodies as he pumped another shell into the chamber.

"Stay there," Ben yelled to Joel while keeping his eye on the men. He gave both bodies a push with his foot when he reached them. The man with the pistol tipped over and rolled limply onto his side. The 12-gauge slug had torn a large hole in his back upon exit, and Ben was forced to step back in order to avoid the ever-expanding pool of blood around the body.

The guy Joel had shot remained motionless when Ben prodded him with the sole of his boot. Joel's two shots to the chest had finished him off, and Ben was impressed with the grouping and accuracy of Joel's shooting, especially considering the adrenaline that was surely coursing through the boy's veins.

Satisfied that these two no longer posed a threat, Ben glanced around to make sure there were no others waiting in the wings. He was proud of Joel for stepping up and taking action, but he was mad that Jack had jumped the gun and potentially put everyone in danger with his spur-of-the-moment shooting. What was Jack thinking? He knew Ben and Joel were outside and that they would handle it. Ben was also a little angry with himself for not acting sooner; he never should have waited so long or let it get this far.

Ben glanced up at the second-floor windows,

but there was no one there. He turned his attention to Joel, who had lowered his pistol by now but remained where he had taken the shots.

"Are you okay?" Ben called out as he ran to Joel's side. "Joel?" Ben raised his voice.

After a few seconds, Joel looked at him. "Yeah... Yeah, I'm fine."

He didn't look fine, and Ben could tell he was in shock.

"I... I had to shoot him. He was going to kill you." Joel shuddered and returned to staring at the body on the ground.

"You did the right thing." Ben put his hand on Joel's shoulder and squeezed, but Joel remained fixated on the bodies and stood there, emotionless. He needed to move his son away from here and then dispose of the bodies.

"Why don't you go check on everybody upstairs?" Ben suggested in the calmest voice he could manage. Joel holstered his gun and started for the steps without saying a word or breaking eye contact with the bodies. But before he could reach the deck, the rear door of the house flung open, and Allie stepped out with a concerned look on her face.

"Jack's been shot!" she yelled. Joel looked back at Ben, and then the two of them ran for the door.

· 15 ·

Ben's mind raced as he followed Allie and Joel into the house and up the stairs. Why couldn't Jack have stayed hidden like he asked? He was about to take the guys out. If Jack had just waited a little longer, they wouldn't be in this position. As they crested the top of the stairs, Ben could see the others gathered on the floor in the rear-facing bedroom.

"What happened?" Ben asked.

"Jack got hit. We were hiding in the closet. He told us to wait in there." Sandy was on the floor next to Jack and had a towel pressed against his waist. Bradley and Emma were nearby and both in tears as they watched their grandfather bleed out in front of their eyes. The towel Sandy was using to stop the bleeding was already soaked through. Both Gunner and Sam paced the room nervously. The dogs knew something was wrong, and Sam whined and grumbled as she stopped to sniff around the wound. Gunner kept his distance and continued to circle the room like he was looking for something.

Ben took over for her and grabbed the towel, then moved it aside quickly to assess the damage. It looked pretty bad. Based on the pieces of glass embedded in Jack's gut, he must have been standing close to the window. He quickly moved the wet towel back over the wound as the blood continued to pump out at an alarming rate. Ben rolled Jack onto his side slightly, and his worst fears were confirmed by the blood spot on the carpet. The bullet had gone all the way through and had done a lot of damage in the process.

"Go get me more towels...and some water," Ben barked. He looked at Jack, who had his eyes closed and was barely breathing. He knew the water and towels were a waste of time considering the amount of blood he had already lost. Even if Jack was in good health, he would have trouble coming back from this.

"Come on, guys. Go get some towels and water," Sandy repeated. Ben wondered if Sandy actually thought there was a chance to save Jack or if she just wanted to spare the kids like he did. Joel had tears in his eyes now, along with Allie and the kids. They all began to reluctantly do as they were told, but Ben didn't have the heart to send them away on a useless errand and have their grandfather pass without them at his side.

"Stay." Ben looked at them as they stopped at the bedroom door and shook his head slowly. He had one hand on the towel and was holding Jack's wrist with the other. His pulse had slowed significantly, and Ben knew it was only a matter of minutes, if that. There was nothing they could do for him except stay by his side.

The kids hurried back over and knelt by their grandfather. Sandy moved back and made way for Emma, who took her place at his side and grabbed her grandfather's hand. Jack's fingers closed around hers as she squeezed lightly. Gunner stopped his nervous pacing and settled down in the corner of the room, as far away as possible, while Sam took a position by Jack's head and lay quietly with his head resting on her front paws.

"We're here, Grandpa. We're all here," Emma said softly. Ben felt Jack grab his arm and tighten his grip to pull Ben close. He leaned down close to Jack and listened intently.

"Take care of them, Ben," Jack muttered and let out a deep breath before his hand fell away. Ben checked for a pulse, but there was none. Jack was gone.

"Grandpa… Grandpa!" Emma shook his arm. "Is he…" She sobbed loudly and was unable to get the rest of her words out.

Ben nodded.

Bradley hugged his sister as they both cried. Ben leaned back on his knees and wiped a tear from his eye. He forced himself up and took a seat on the bed as he stared at Jack in total disbelief. He knew Jack's time was limited because of the cancer, but that didn't make it any easier to accept what just happened. Less than an hour ago, they were talking in his bedroom.

A sense of guilt washed over Ben like a wave crashing on the beach. He had been so upset with Jack for taking the early shot and, even before that, making him keep his secret about his health from the kids. And now here he was, lying dead on the bedroom floor. None of that mattered anymore. Ben felt foolish and petty for wasting time worrying about what were now trivial things.

He looked at his younger two as they made their way to him and threw themselves onto him and the bed. He wrapped them in his arms and held them tightly for a while before Bradley pulled away to look back at his grandfather. Ben looked over at Joel and saw that he had his face buried in Allie's shoulder. She was holding him tightly. Sandy looked over at Ben and wiped her eyes.

"I'm sorry," she whispered.

All Ben could manage was another nod as he watched the children come to terms with what had happened. It was a lot to take in, especially for Bradley and Emma, who had been living with Jack, but Ben was worried. He wanted to get back outside and make sure the two guys were alone.

He felt vulnerable with all of them up on the second floor. This was the perfect opportunity for someone to take advantage of them.

The kids started to regain their composure and gather around Jack's body. Sandy moved in close behind Emma and Bradley, putting her arms on each of their shoulders. Ben was surprised to see them both lean into her and accept her embrace so readily. But Sandy was a kind-hearted person, and it showed in how she had befriended them all since their arrival at Jack's place. The kids had quickly warmed up to her and Allie, and Ben was especially grateful for that right now. He was glad she and Allie were here. This would be a lot harder to deal with if it was just him and the kids. No doubt they would've preferred their mother by their side, but Sandy was as good of a substitute as he could hope for right now.

Ben felt comfortable leaving them with Sandy, but not before he yanked a comforter off the bed and covered Jack up to his neck. He wanted to give the kids a chance to say their goodbyes, but there was no need to leave his wounds exposed.

"I need to go check outside and make sure it's secure. We don't know if those guys were alone or working with a group."

Joel pulled away from Allie and stood up straight as Ben headed out of the room. He took a big breath. "I can help."

Ben stopped and looked at his son. He debated whether he wanted Joel to be a part of moving the bodies but decided it probably didn't matter at this point.

"You can stay here with your brother and sister if you want," Ben suggested. "I can handle it on my own."

Emma looked up. "We're fine, Dad. You might need Joel out there."

Ben wondered if they had seen what happened in the back yard, but he wasn't about to ask her if she had seen her brother shoot a man. As Ben looked around the room, he realized then and there that his kids were growing up fast. In Joel's case, he was already grown. Not so much in age but in experience and innocence lost. There was no going back, and no matter what the future held, they would never be the same again.

· 16 ·

"All right, come on. We'll be right back." Ben looked around at everyone in the room before heading downstairs with Joel close behind. He wanted to say something to Joel, to impart some words of wisdom or comfort about the shooting and about his grandfather, but he drew a blank. Nothing that popped into his head sounded right, and he didn't want to risk treating Joel like a kid. What do you say to a teenager who just killed a man in self-defense and lost his grandfather within the span of a few minutes?

Ben stopped halfway through the kitchen and turned to face Joel.

"Thanks for saving my butt out there earlier." Ben put his hand on Joel's shoulder and squeezed. "You don't have to do this, you know, help me move the bodies."

"I know, but I want to. Besides, there might be more of them out there." For a moment, Joel paused and gazed out the kitchen window with a faraway look in his eye. "I got your back, Dad." Joel hugged him quickly and wiped his eyes one more time before pulling out his Glock.

"I know you do." Ben shot Joel a crooked smile and headed for the back door. As bad as the situation was, Ben had never been prouder of his son than he was in this moment. In his eyes, there was no denying that Joel was no longer a teenager. It wasn't the first time Joel had been forced to kill, and it most likely wouldn't be his last. Joel was a man now, and Ben vowed then and there to treat him like nothing less. He would always do everything in his power to protect his son, but it was time to let him come into his own.

Ben wasn't sure if the two guys in the Chevy were alone, but he wasn't taking any chances. And even if it was just the two of them, the shooting might have attracted some unwanted attention. If it had been earlier in the day, Ben might have considered hastily loading the trucks and getting out of there within the hour. But it was too late for that, and by the time they finished, there would only be a few hours of travel time before dark. It also felt a lot like running, and that didn't sit well with him, either.

They would stick to the plan and leave in the morning. They needed to pack quickly and efficiently, but he didn't want to rush through it and risk forgetting something crucial. It wouldn't take that long to finish gearing up the trucks tonight, and if it cooled down a little, they could get it all done in a couple of hours.

In addition to preparing the trucks for the long trip ahead, they were now faced with an additional task, one Ben wasn't looking forward to: what to do with Jack's body. He hated to even think about it, but it had to be done. They would give Jack a proper burial under the old magnolia tree. That was what Jack wanted, and it was the least they could do for him.

Digging the grave would be backbreaking work in the dry, hard ground, but it needed to happen, especially for the kids. They needed a clean start to the trip, and this would hopefully give them some measure of closure. The journey would be hard enough without carrying the burden of guilt and the thought of Jack wrapped up in a blanket and lying in the bedroom. Morale would already be at an all-time low, and Ben wanted to give them the best chance possible to make it home.

He and Joel made their way onto the back deck, and Ben scanned the surrounding fields for any signs of movement. They held still for a while and listened for any sounds, but there was nothing other than the occasional breeze rustling rows of dead soybeans.

Ben noticed a slight change in the temperature. The sun was beginning to creep westward, and several darker clouds had formed in the sky since the last time he was outside. The shade they provided gave welcome relief from the relentless sunlight they'd grown accustomed to.

"Do you think it's going to rain?" Joel asked.

"It sure looks like it." Ben didn't want to get his hopes up, but there was no denying that those were storm clouds and an ever-darkening horizon to the east. They were less than twenty miles from the Atlantic Ocean, and Ben was excited about the prospects of a system moving in from the coast. Not because they needed the rain. Everything here was already dead or dying anyway, but maybe the storm was the beginning of weather patterns returning to something close to normal. If nothing else, it would break the heat, and although he felt a bit morbid for thinking this, it would soften the ground a little.

"It'd be nice to see some rain for a change," Joel said. "It's been a while."

"That it has. The last rain we saw was in Colorado." Ben stopped focusing on the weather and resumed his assessment of the property.

"Let's take a walk around, just to be safe." Ben held the KSG across his torso and started down the steps. He looked over at the bodies. They were still in the same awkward positions as when he last saw them. He wasn't sure what he expected, but he was glad to see them unchanged. He noticed Joel stealing glances at the two dead men as well, but he remained silent.

They made their way around the house first, careful to take their time and move slowly, especially across the front of the property, where they were visible from the road. Confident the front was clear, Ben led them to the north side and up the driveway, past the house, and back to the outbuilding. Once they had checked the perimeter of the garage and the fields beyond, they were confident they were alone once more.

"Maybe it was just the two of them," Joel said.

"Maybe." Ben sighed. He wasn't about to let his guard down, and he probably wouldn't feel good about things until they were back on the road again.

There was no putting off what had to be done next. Thankfully, Jack's tractor was still running, and it had a set of forks on the front end. It would have been nice if it was equipped with a bucket. That would have made digging a grave for Jack a lot easier, but Ben had no intention of providing such luxuries for the two thieves.

He and Joel opened up the garage, and Ben found the keys in the tractor's ignition. The old John Deere fired right up, and after taking a couple of seconds to look over the controls, Ben drove into the yard. The forks were already close together, so there was no need to adjust them, and he had no problem getting under the already slightly stiff bodies with the long metal forks. In hindsight, he could have done this without Joel, but an extra set of eyes and ears while he was running the tractor and distracted was a good idea.

With both bodies on board, he slowed the throttle and yelled over to Joel, who was watching him.

"I'm going to take them back into the field aways. I'll be right back. Keep an eye out here, okay?"

Joel nodded and gave him a thumbs-up as he drove past and headed into the brown sea of soybeans. He glanced back when he was a few hundred yards away and saw that Joel was inspecting the rifle that the fat man had leaned against the building.

Ben drove a little farther, and when he was sure the bodies would be out of sight, he pushed the lever forward and watched them slide off the forks. They tumbled over each other as they hit the ground and kicked up a small cloud of dust. Ben was tempted to call it done and cut the wheel hard to the right. He was about to turn around and drive back, but instead, he put the tractor in neutral and throttled down to a low idle. Hopping down from the seat, he landed hard on the ground. The dirt out here between the planted rows was rock-hard, and it felt like he was on pavement.

It wouldn't take long, but he wanted to get the pistol. The fat man had nothing on him that Ben cared about, but the other man had a pistol that might be useful, depending on the caliber. It was still in the man's hand, and he was surprised it hadn't fallen out on the bumpy ride out here. Ben pried the gun from his hand, which was still surprisingly flexible, and examined it. He had mixed emotions about the weapon, seeing as how it was the gun that killed Jack. But the pragmatist in him knew that it was just a gun and that it was in fact the man who had killed Jack.

It was a dull gray Springfield 1911-style .45 semiautomatic pistol. The gun was in good condition and had been taken care of. It was a newer model, probably not more than a few years old. Part of Ben wanted it to be a piece of junk so he could strip it of ammunition and leave it to rust in the field, but it wasn't, and they had plenty of .45-caliber ammunition, thanks to Jack. They needed to keep the gun.

When Ben climbed back up onto the tractor, he used an old towel Jack kept tied to the seat and a little spit to remove a spot of blood from the handle on the pistol. He definitely couldn't bring the gun back like that. Satisfied it would pass inspection, he tucked it into his belt and headed back.

As he approached the outbuilding, he noticed that Joel had a shovel in his hands and was busy working. Only when Ben was closer did he realized what he was doing. He had covered the bloodstains on the ground with loose dirt from around the yard. Ben parked the tractor in the garage and shut it down. Joel was using the shovel handle to prop himself up and had already worked up a sweat.

Joel shrugged. "Just cleaning up a little. Didn't want Bradley or Emma to see that."

"Good thinking. I was wondering how we were going to clean that up." The stains were near the entrance to the garage and right on the path to the house. Ben didn't want the constant reminder about the day's events while they were loading the trucks tonight.

Ben stopped in the shade next to Joel and rested for a minute against the building. It was cooling down, but the humidity was still brutal. The shovel made Ben think about the task ahead of them, and he glanced over at the magnolia tree in the far corner of the once-manicured yard.

Joel was looking at the tree now, too. "Are we going to bury Grandpa there?"

"I think we should. It's what he wanted."

"That's where Grandma is, right?"

"Yeah, her ashes were spread there. You were pretty young then."

"Then I think we should bury him there, too." Joel looked down at the ground for a second and cleared his throat. "We owe him that much."

Ben nodded. "That we do, son. That we do."

· 17 ·

Ben and Joel stood quietly and watched the clouds for a minute. Ben could have stayed there and let his mind drift with the clouds, but they needed to rejoin the others inside and help.

A strange peaceful feeling washed over him, or maybe it was a sense of relief. He no longer had to keep Jack's secret to himself. It was a burden lifted from his conscience. Not that he would've ever hoped for this, but it was a release nonetheless.

He made up his mind to tell the kids the truth about Jack and what he was facing in the near future. Maybe it would be easier for them to cope with his death if they really knew what was going on with his health. After all, Jack was surrounded by loved ones when he passed. If they left him here like Jack wanted, he would have died alone and probably in a lot of pain. Hopefully the kids would see it that way, too.

"We better get back inside and help the others." Ben smacked Joel on the shoulder and started closing the doors on the outbuilding.

"Yeah, I guess you're right." Joel was still looking up at the forming clouds and reluctantly put the shovel away so he could help his dad lock up. Ben sensed Joel's hesitation to go back inside, and he didn't blame him one bit. There wasn't anything to look forward to in the house, where they were going to have to deal with Jack's body along with some tough emotional issues.

Once the garage was secure and Ben moved the Chevy pickup the two guys were driving around to the back side of the outbuilding, he and Joel headed inside. As soon as they opened the door, Gunner was there to greet them, his tail beating the wall loudly as it wagged with excitement. Ben wondered where Sam was. The dogs had been inseparable since everyone arrived the other day.

The house smelled of dog and cigar smoke, not to mention a few other things that made it feel grim. The closed curtains didn't help with the overall cave-like feeling, and Ben's newly gained optimism from his time outside with Joel began to fade. The main thing he noticed, though, was how hot and stuffy it had become inside the house. The coolness of the air-conditioning had long since worn off, and for the first time in a while, it felt better outside than in.

Everyone was gathered in the living room now, sitting quietly and no doubt in deep thought about all that had happened. When Ben and Joel entered, no one moved or said a word. They were all in a daze and in desperate need of some fresh air in the house. The staleness of the room was oppressive, and in the chaos of the afternoon, no one had thought to open the windows again.

Ben opened the front door a few inches and had Joel crack a window. The effect was immediate, and a fresh breeze flowed through the room, getting everyone's attention. Emma was the first one up and ran over to both of them with open arms. She caught Ben off guard and squeezed hard as she hung on. Bradley wasn't far behind and joined in on the group hug. Allie came over next and stood by Joel with her arms around him and Emma. Sandy followed, and they all stayed huddled together for a minute or two.

Ben hated to break it up, but he felt the urge to get moving. The world they lived in didn't allow for the luxury of mourning Jack's passing for days or even hours. It would be easy to mope around here for the rest of the night while they tried to process everything that had happened, but they couldn't afford to do that. He didn't expect anyone to get over it quickly, especially the children, but they would have to be sad while they were productive if they were to make it out of here tomorrow morning. He also wanted to take advantage of the cooler temperatures while they lasted.

The front that was moving in had dropped the temperature outside a good fifteen degrees, and Ben saw no reason why they should wait any longer to start making final preparations to the vehicles. If they could get a head start, it would allow them extra time to rest tonight. It would also be a lot easier to organize the trucks and gear while they had daylight. Not having to use lights outside at night would also make him feel less exposed.

After what happened today, he had no intention of leaving the house vulnerable to any intruders. He was planning on staying up part of the night and keeping watch. Between him, Sandy, Joel, and Allie, they could take turns standing watch throughout the night. If they could each do a couple hours apiece, they should still be able to get enough rest to have a productive day of travel tomorrow.

They also needed extra time to tend to the burial. He considered digging the grave right now and getting Jack in the ground sooner rather than later, but it didn't feel right, and he was afraid it would be too much too fast for the kids. Besides, with any luck, they would get a little rain and the ground would loosen up. Ben thought about the rock-hard dirt in the soybean field and shuddered at the thought of burning himself out digging a large enough hole for Jack.

As they all loosened their grips on one another and backed away from the group hug, Ben thought it might be as good a time as any to level with everyone about Jack's condition. It might help ease their sorrow in some small way, and it would make him feel better to get it over with and off his chest.

"I need to tell you guys something about your grandpa." Everyone stopped and listened to Ben. "You all know Grandpa was sick, but he was more than just sick. He was... Well, he was dying." Ben paused to look at each one of his kids as well as Allie and her mother. They all had the same confused expression.

"What do you mean?" Joel asked. "He was dying? Like, soon?"

"Yeah, that's the real reason he didn't want to come with us. He wasn't sure how much longer he had, but he was convinced it would be any day now. He ran out of his medicine a while ago and he felt like things were getting worse fast. He didn't want us to have to deal with that, and he didn't want to use valuable resources that we might need." Ben paused as he scanned their faces for a reaction.

"What was wrong with him?" Bradley asked.

"Cancer," Emma answered.

Ben was surprised to hear her say that. He had no idea she knew that much.

She looked down at the floor in an effort to avoid the stares. "I heard Grandpa and Mom talking a few weeks ago."

"She's right," Ben confirmed. "I don't know the details, but he'd been fighting it for some time now."

"I would have wanted him to come with us anyway," Joel said, raising his voice. "I wish you had told us sooner, while he was alive."

"He made me swear not to say a word. It was his last wish for me to keep it secret. Believe me, I tried on more than one occasion to convince him to come with us, but you know your grandpa. Once he makes up his mind about something, that's it."

"I had a feeling there was more to it than that," Sandy chimed in. "He really didn't look well. I noticed a difference in him the short time we were here."

"He hung in there and tried to keep up appearances for as long as he could. He didn't want you guys to worry, but when we got here, he knew you were in good hands and he could let go. What happened was a terrible thing, and I'm sad, just like you guys are, but try to think of this. Your grandpa loved you all very much, and he died protecting us. That's what he would have wanted, given the circumstances. It may not be much of a consolation, but he was surrounded by family when he passed. I, for one, think that's a far better option than him hanging on by a thread here after we left and then dying all alone." It took Ben all he had not to choke on the words.

"I guess that's why he wanted us to take Sam," Bradley added.

"That's right, buddy. Your grandpa always put others before himself, even old Sam." Ben was glad to see that the kids were thinking about this in a positive light. Or at least that was what he hoped.

"We're going to bury him tonight out under the tree by Grandma. Dad and I will dig the hole later," Joel said. "It's what Grandpa wanted."

"I can help," Allie offered.

"Me too," Sandy added. "That's going to be a lot of work."

Ben felt like he had given the kids enough information for now and thought it was a good time to change the conversation.

"Thanks, but first I want to get the trucks packed and the gear sorted through. The plan is to get up early tomorrow, have breakfast, and get on the road."

"Allie and I will go through the food and take inventory of what we have," Sandy said.

"We should go through the kitchen first," Allie added. "There's no sense in leaving anything behind that might be useful."

"Good thinking," Ben said.

"Me and Bradley can help, too," Emma offered.

"Good. We can get it all done if everybody chips in. Joel and I will get started sorting out the guns and ammo. Grandpa gave me most of the stuff from his safe." Ben glanced at Joel. "Maybe you can give me a hand with it."

"Sure."

"All right. I guess that's it for now. Let's get to it. Oh, one other thing. Let's open some windows and let some fresh air in here. It will do us all some good, and it's actually pretty decent out right now." As the group broke up and went to work opening windows, Ben motioned for Joel to follow him to Jack's bedroom. Halfway down the hall, he stopped.

"I'll meet you in there in a minute. I just want to check on something. Maybe you can get started separating the ammo," Ben asked as he passed Joel and headed upstairs. He would have preferred to join Joel in the bedroom rather than do what he was about to do.

Ben wanted to wrap up Jack's body and move him to the outbuilding. It was still going to be warm in the house, even with the windows open and especially upstairs. Not exactly ideal conditions to keep a body. He thought it would be best to get Jack out of the house for the kids' sake. It would be better for morale, too. No one was about to forget what happened, but they didn't need a constant reminder looming nearby.

When Ben reached the top of the stairway, he was greeted by a subdued Sam, who wagged her tail briefly but remained seated by the closed bedroom door. He felt sorry for the dog and knelt to scratch her head.

"Hey there, Sam. I'm sorry, girl, but don't you worry. We'll take good care of you. I promise." Ben continued stroking Sam's neck as he spoke. Sam's eyes closed as she sat, solemnly guarding the door and basking in the attention Ben was giving her. The poor dog. Ben was pretty sure Sam knew exactly what was going on or at least that Jack was gone. A tear welled in his eye, and Ben felt a little silly for talking to the dog, but the feeling quickly passed when Sam leaned in and buried her face in Ben's chest.

"It'll be okay, girl. Everything's going to be okay." Ben wasn't sure if he was saying that for the dog's benefit or his.

· 18 ·

Ben took another minute with Sam and regained his composure before he entered the bedroom. He expected Sam to follow him, but the dog remained at the door, watching his every move. To his surprise, Jack's body was fully covered now, neatly wrapped in the comforter from head to toe. Sandy or Allie must have done it before they all went downstairs.

"I hope you don't mind. I covered him up while Allie took the kids downstairs." Sandy startled Ben. He hadn't noticed her standing in the doorway. "Sorry," she added. "I just came up to open some windows."

"No, it's fine. Thanks. I'm going to move him out of the house while the kids are busy," Ben replied.

"I think that's a good idea. They're in the kitchen helping Allie right now. I'll help you go out the front."

Ben was surprised by how light Jack's body was, a testament to how much his health had deteriorated. When Ben thought of Jack, he had the image of a man who was always busy around the house, fixing something or out back splitting wood for the winter ahead. In a way, Ben was glad Jack's pain and suffering were over. Although he felt a little selfish for thinking this way, he was glad that the kids wouldn't have to worry about him here by himself. It would be a load off of his mind. The thought of leaving Jack here had bothered him a lot, and the image of him wasting away all alone in this house would have haunted him all the way back to Colorado and beyond.

Fortunately, the kids were busy helping Allie in the kitchen, and with Sandy's help, he was able to slip out with the body unnoticed. Ben made his way off the porch while making sure to keep an eye out for any activity. Sam followed this time. Once they were outside, she seemed to be in better spirits, stopping to smell the breeze from time to time. Sam investigated the spots Joel had covered with dirt to camouflage the blood-soaked ground while Ben placed the body in the back corner of the garage and covered it with a tarp.

"Come on, Sam. Let's go." Ben called out as he locked up and hurried back to the house. He wanted to get back to Joel and help him with the ammo. But more than that, he wanted to give Joel the 1911. It was a shame Jack didn't have the chance to give it to Joel himself.

The house felt better already and lacked the dark, dank atmosphere it had when Ben first came inside with Joel a little while ago. The curtains were still drawn, allowing some light through, and the breeze moved around them now as well. He opened the door wide to let Sam scoot past him as she ran to greet Gunner, who was ready and waiting for his new friend. Gunner sniffed Sam from head to tail before the two disappeared into the living room with one of Sam's rope toys.

Ben was glad to see a little life return to the old dog. Sam was no puppy, and Ben was concerned that between her age and the loss of Jack, she might not fully recover.

Sandy was in the kitchen, helping Allie and the kids. They had the contents of Jack's cabinets and pantry spread out on the counters and kitchen table.

"We may have more than we can carry," Allie quipped.

"If it's worth taking, we'll find a way." Ben winked as he passed through on his way to Jack's bedroom. They would, too; with extra mouths to feed, it was important to take all they could fit and more. He'd figure out a way to lash stuff on the roof of the Jeep if he had to.

Joel was making good progress sorting the ammunition and had started a list with quantities of each caliber. Ben was happy to see him hard at work. It was a good way to get his mind off all the bad things and work through his emotions. But it wasn't the real reason he wanted to get Joel alone for a minute or two.

"Making good progress, I see."

Joel looked over the various piles on the floor. "Yeah. Grandpa sure had a lot of ammo."

"I guess you could say your grandpa was a bit of a prepper."

"Well, that's good for us, right?"

"For sure." Ben turned to look for Jack's .45. He found it on the bench at the foot of the bed.

"Here you go. Grandpa wanted you to have that. He was going to give it to you himself before we left tomorrow."

"Really? Wow!" Joel took the pistol from his dad and slowly drew it from the holster. He walked over to the window and pulled the curtain aside to let more light in and inspect the intricate scrollwork that adorned both sides of the custom pistol. Joel studied the .45 for a minute more before putting it back in the holster and looking over at his dad. His eyes were red and he was fighting off tears.

"Well, I better finish up with the ammo so we can get it loaded up." Joel struggled to get the words out smoothly.

"I'm sorry I didn't tell you about your grandpa's health sooner. I should have been upfront with you," Ben said.

Joel nodded. "It's okay, Dad. I understand."

Ben wasn't sure if he really did understand, but maybe someday he would. He didn't like keeping things from Joel, and in hindsight, he wished he had been upfront with him about what was going on with Jack.

"Come on. I'll help you with the rest of this." Eager to change the subject, Ben took a spot on the floor and started sorting through the rest of the ammunition. It didn't take long to get it organized into piles of what they would keep out for easy access in each vehicle and what they would pack away under more crucial supplies.

They would be traveling with a well-stocked armory for the return trip, and from the looks of the kitchen, the MREs in the outbuilding, and what they already had, they would have plenty of food as well. If they had trouble getting home, it wouldn't be due to a lack of supplies.

Seeing the piles of gear come together put Ben's mind at ease a little. Providing enough resources for all these people was one of his main concerns from the start. That wasn't to say he still didn't have plenty to worry about. Beyond their control were a lot of other factors that they would surely encounter along the way. He tried to remain optimistic, but the reality was that they would see more of what they'd run into on the trip here. No one thought the trip back would be easy, but thinking it wouldn't be just as dangerous was foolish.

Things weren't getting any easier out there, and there would be more desperate people willing to do anything to survive. The ones who had managed to endure the hardships of this new world for this long would present a more formidable challenge. They would be the ones with the skills and the tenacity it took to withstand these dire conditions. The survivors who had held out this long because they had supplies and had been in hiding until now would soon be out and about.

Even the amateur preppers who considered themselves prepared and somewhat resourceful would be wearing thin by now. The stakes would be higher, and people driven by hunger and desperation would be bolder in their attempts to take what they needed. Ben couldn't afford to underestimate any person or group he encountered on the road, and he wouldn't. There would be no more giving folks the benefit of the doubt. As far as Ben was concerned, everyone was suspect and would be considered hostile until proven otherwise.

It meant more cold-camping; the luxury of a fire would be too risky. Even using the smokeless method wasn't foolproof, and they would have to play it safe unless they were absolutely sure no one was around. They'd utilize the use of the gas stoves for as long as the fuel held out. Even then, there was the risk of someone smelling them or whatever they were cooking.

Both vehicles had four-wheel drive and were capable off-road rigs. Maybe it was time to use them more in that regard. Moving off the road farther during the night, or even when they rested during the heat of the day, would be worth the effort if it meant avoiding trouble.

There were also more of them now, and that meant more responsibility on him. Joel and Allie were capable and had come a long way since they pulled out of Durango that first morning, and from what he'd seen so far, Sandy was no slouch when it came to pulling her own weight. She seemed more than happy to do her share to help out, and although unproven, she claimed to know how to use a gun. But even when he took all this into consideration, he still felt responsible for the group's well-being. If anything happened to any one of them, he'd never be able to forgive himself.

· 19 ·

With the ammunition sorted and ready to load into the trucks, Ben and Joel headed into the kitchen. It was getting close to dinnertime, and the darkening sky made it seem even later. When they entered the kitchen, Ben could see that Sandy and the kids were wrapping up their efforts in there as well.

"Everything okay?" Allie eyed the AR-15 Ben was carrying. It was the one with the nice Trijicon scope from Jack's safe. Ben had loaded up a couple of magazines for it and had intended to keep it in the living room, along with the KSG, for the time being, just in case.

"Sorry, yeah. I just wanted to keep this out here for easy access if there was any more trouble." Ben felt bad for coming out into the living room while loaded to the hilt with guns. He imagined how it must have appeared, and by the looks on Bradley's and Emma's faces, he realized that Allie wasn't the only one he had alarmed.

"I was going to start dinner. Do you want me to use the camp stove or should we use the generator to power the range?" Sandy asked.

Ben thought about it for a second while he peeked through the living room window once more for any signs of life. He didn't see anything outside. They might as well take advantage of the generator while they had it. He wanted to make more ice to help keep the deer meat in Jack's freezer from spoiling, and he also wanted extra for the coolers they were taking with them in the morning.

"Yeah, why not? I guess it's time to pull the trucks out and get them ready."

"We've only got a couple more hours of daylight if we're lucky, and it's getting darker out early with the incoming storm," Joel mentioned.

"Okay, Joel and I can get started, and then everyone can help out after dinner."

"Can I come out with you guys?" Bradley asked.

"Sure," Joel answered before Ben had a chance to think about it, but he didn't have the heart to tell Bradley no. And he didn't want to scare the kids anymore by telling them that he was worried someone would retaliate for the men they had killed. He was pretty sure the intruders weren't alone. Neither of the guys seemed like they had the smarts to make it this far on their own.

"Give me a minute and I'll have the generator up and running." Ben kept the AR-15 and leaned the KSG up against the wall between the kitchen and living room. They had weapons in the Blazer if they ran into any trouble outside, but he wanted the Trijicon ACOG scope with them. Even with limited light outside, he'd be able to see clearly across the field thanks to the tritium fiber optic-illuminated reticle. It wasn't night vision by any stretch, but it was the next best thing.

"I'm leaving the shotgun here for you guys, just in case. It's loaded and the safety is on," Ben announced. He knew Allie had her shotgun handy and hoped that Sandy was keeping the .38 nearby, but having a little extra protection couldn't hurt. It did give Ben an idea, though: maybe tomorrow, before they left, they should do a little shooting. It would be a good opportunity to make sure everyone could operate the various weapons they had.

It wouldn't matter if the shooting drew any attention from people nearby. It wouldn't take long to give everyone a crash course on the new guns and practice a little with the ones they carried. As long as they were all packed up and ready to pull out, they would be gone by the time anyone came to investigate. A half-hour or so of range time was a small price to pay for peace of mind and knowing that, if and when the time came to fight, they would be ready.

Ben held the door wide open. "We're taking the dogs with us." Gunner and Sam took the cue and bolted out the door like it was the first time they'd ever been let out of the house. The dogs flew down the steps and began to chase each other around the yard in tight circles. Sam seemed to have forgotten about Jack for the time being. Either that or the cooler weather and Gunner's persistence had finally persuaded her to play.

Bradley and Joel followed their dad outside, and the three paused for a minute on the back deck. The temperature had dropped even more, and it actually felt nice out for a change. Ben was glad they waited to organize and pack the trucks.

"Can I see that?" Joel asked as he admired the AR-15.

"Sure." Ben handed him the rifle.

"I just want to look through the scope for a second."

"You might as well hang onto it for now and keep an eye out while you're at it. I'll get the garage opened up so we can move the trucks out after I start the generator." Ben left the boys on the deck and headed down into the yard, all the while keeping an eye out himself.

If it wasn't for Jack's death, he'd be feeling pretty good about things right now. He had all of his kids, and they were heading home tomorrow with more supplies than he'd ever hoped for. It had been good to recharge here for a night or two, but he was anxious to get back on the road.

The outbuilding was dark, and Ben used his flashlight to find his way to the generator and start it up. He wished it was in a separate room that he could close off. It was loud in the garage, and once he pulled the Blazer and Jeep outside, he would have to close the doors so they wouldn't broadcast the sound.

Ben flipped the switch and turned it off. On second thought, he decided to move all the gear out before starting up the generator. He feared he was becoming too comfortable again. He knew all too well what letting your guard down for even a second could lead to.

Ben threw the large overhead door open in front of the Jeep and the supplies they had compiled from the garage shelves. "Hey, Joel, how about letting Bradley take over and come give me a hand?"

"Coming." Joel handed Bradley the AR and joined his dad. They moved the Jeep and Blazer out into the driveway behind the house and close to the back deck, along with whatever else they were going to pack up. Once the building was closed up again, Ben started the generator and gave Bradley a thumbs-up so he could let the girls know they had power now.

Bradley seemed happy to be assigned watch duties from the deck while Ben and Joel started going through the trucks. Ben kept checking on him, and every time he looked over, Bradley was busy scanning the property through the scope.

Ben and Joel discussed the driving arrangements, and Joel was fine with having Allie and Gunner in the Jeep with him, not that Ben was surprised by that, although Joel was sure to get a light-hearted jab in about his dad stealing his truck out from under him.

Allie and Emma made their way outside and down to the garden to cut a few zucchinis off the vine for dinner.

"We'll be ready to eat in about ten minutes," Allie called out on their way back inside.

"I think we should eat outside tonight," Joel yelled back.

"Okay, it is pretty nice out," Allie agreed as she and Emma disappeared into the house, leaving the back door open this time. Before Ben knew it, the girls were carrying out plates and a jug of tea. He turned the generator off for the time being, and they all found a spot to sit around the trucks. They sat in silence for a while as everyone devoured their meals and listened to the distant thunder that was now becoming more frequent.

Gunner and Sam had long since calmed down and focused their efforts on looking pitiful in hopes of scoring some leftovers. They were both happy to find out that there was a venison steak, complete with the bone, for both of them. There was no point in letting it go to waste, and now that they wouldn't be leaving any behind for Jack, there was more than they would get to before it spoiled.

Ben planned on taking as much of it with them as they could. Even when they ran out of ice and it started to spoil, the dogs could stomach it for a day or two longer than they could. It wouldn't be pretty, but it meant being able to save the dried and canned food for when they didn't have any other options. There were two dogs now, and although Jack had a large bag of dry food for Sam, it would only go so far. They had plenty of food for themselves and the dogs, but Ben was too conservative to not give it some thought. It was fine to give the dogs leftovers, but he didn't want to be in a position where they had to start sharing rice with them.

There were some leftovers, and the dogs lucked out again with a small portion of rice and zucchini for each of them. With dinner finished and cleaned up, they all chipped in and began to work at packing the trucks. The kids all worked together: using the hand truck, they made several trips back and forth to the house, shuttling supplies to Ben and Sandy, who in turn stowed them in the vehicles. They were careful to leave plenty of room for Gunner in the Jeep and for Sam in the Blazer.

Ben was actually surprised at how well everything fit, and he felt good about the load in each vehicle. He was careful to make sure each vehicle had all the supplies to be self-sufficient if need be. He hoped it wouldn't come to that, and he couldn't fathom any scenario in which they would willfully split up. But he knew all too well that he had to plan for more than just what they anticipated.

After triple-checking and going over the inventory, they were done, at least as far as they could go tonight. There would be some clothes and a few last-minute things to pack in the morning, but overall, they were ready to hit the road tomorrow.

Ben kept out extra ammunition and let them all know his thoughts about getting in a little range time first thing tomorrow. Everyone agreed, and the kids seemed excited at the prospect of shooting the guns before they settled in for what would be a long, hard day of driving. Ben was glad to see them enthusiastic about something and it was a welcome change of conversation as they talked among themselves about the trip. It was the first time since the incident with Jack that the cloud of depression hanging over them all seemed to lift, even if just a little.

Ben didn't have the heart to stop them from going inside when they were finished. Only Sandy remained outside with him, and once the kids were gone, he pulled two beers out of the cooler, partly because it would be a long time before he had a chance to enjoy a cold beer again, but mostly because he wanted to dull his senses a little for the task ahead. There was no more putting it off. It was time to dig Jack's grave. Joel said he would help, but Ben was reluctant to pull him back into reality just yet.

· 20 ·

Sandy helped him pull the trucks back into the garage. Between moving the vehicles and looking for shovels, Ben could hear the kids' voices carry into the back yard. It sounded like they were playing a card game, and while he was glad they were content and preoccupied with something other than the end of the world and their grandpa's death, he was worried someone might hear them.

"I think maybe it's time to close up the house. I'll run the generator in a bit, and we can turn the air on tonight. Plus, we should close the curtains again if they're going to be using lights."

"Okay, I'll let them know." Sandy set her beer down and headed in while Ben continued searching for something to make digging the hole a little easier. He couldn't help but glance over at the tarp occasionally as he rummaged through Jack's tools. He finished his drink, set the empty bottle on the workbench, and stared for a second at the old metal John Deere sign on the wall. Then he remembered seeing a few implements for the tractor around the back side of the outbuilding. He hadn't paid much attention earlier when he moved the bodies, but it was worth a look.

Ben wandered around back and took a look around with his flashlight. A few implements were half-buried in the tall grass, and among them was a post-hole digger. He was hoping for a small backhoe attachment or even a bucket, but this would do. The post-hole digger wouldn't remove the dirt, but it would at least break up the ground and save his back. Though they'd have to remove the dirt with the shovels, it would be half the work. He felt bad for thinking like this, but anything that would get this over with sooner was good with him. If he hurried, he could get it dug before it was too dark to see.

There was currently a landscape box attached to the rear of the tractor. Jack used it for grading the driveway and keeping the gravel in place. Ben wasn't familiar with the three-point hitch setup on the tractor, but when Sandy came back from the house, they put their heads together and figured it out. He used the forks to pull the post-hole digger out of the overgrown weeds and bring it around front. Sandy helped him line it up with the implement, and within a few minutes, they had it hooked up and operational.

The implement worked well and made short work of the dry, hard ground. Fortunately, the shade of the tree had spared the area underneath from becoming sun-baked and rock-hard like the field out back. It still took a little while to get the area broken up and ready for the shovels, but mostly because he stopped every few minutes to take a look around.

Operating the auger required him to rev up the RPMs on the tractor in order to get enough power to the PTO, and he was afraid he was making too much noise. But so far there was no sign of any activity out on the road—or anywhere else, for that matter. Ben was beginning to think that maybe the two men they'd killed were in fact on their own.

Once he'd done as much as he could with the tractor, he parked it at the back of the outbuilding and started the generator before locking everything up again. Sandy was already hard at work shoveling the loose dirt out of the hole, and Ben grabbed a shovel to join her. Within a few minutes, Joel and Allie had joined them.

"I figured you guys were out here working on this. I told you I would help," Joel said.

"I know, but I didn't want to pull you away from your brother and sister. They need you right now more than ever. Besides, I was able to use the tractor to do the hard part."

Joel looked back at the house. "They didn't want to come out for this."

"I understand." Ben didn't blame them but hoped they would join them when the time came to put Jack in the ground. He wouldn't force them to participate, but he thought it would be good for them to get closure. But they were still kids, as hard as that was to remember at times, given what they had already been through, so whatever they wanted to do would be fine with him.

Joel and Allie took over shoveling dirt for a while. There were only two shovels, so they rotated as they worked, except for Joel, who seemed determined to dig the entire hole on his own. Ben wasn't sure if he was showing off for Allie's sake or just being his usual stubborn self. There was also the possibility that he was releasing a little pent-up anger over what had happened to Jack. Or maybe he was still upset that Ben had kept the truth about Jack's health from him. He hoped that wasn't the case, but there was nothing Ben could do about that now if it was.

They worked in silence as they dug, aside from the occasional word or two when they exchanged shovels and Ben's pleas for Joel to take a break. He didn't want Joel to wear himself out. They had a long drive ahead of them tomorrow, and with Joel and Allie basically being on their own in the Jeep, they would need to be at the top of their game.

Ben wasn't looking forward to the drive himself, and the thought of getting back on the road tomorrow was bittersweet. It was a necessary evil if they were going to make it back to Colorado, but it didn't make it any more enjoyable. His back was just starting to feel normal, and he really wasn't looking forward to sleeping on the ground again.

Ben promised himself he would try to be less of a control freak and let Sandy share in the driving, if she was so inclined. Based on her willingness to help out with pretty much everything else they'd done up to this point, he was sure she would offer sooner rather than later, and he was okay with that. Or at least that was what he told himself.

The dynamic of the trip would be different this time. With Bradley and Emma joining them, he would have to be more dad and less commando. For the most part, the older kids were self-sufficient, and he didn't feel the need to make unnecessary small talk, but with Bradley and Emma, he felt a certain responsibility to constantly water things down. They were smart kids, and he assumed for the most part they understood what was going on around them. But he still felt the desire to shelter them as much as he could. He didn't see that changing anytime soon.

It was a feeling he'd been forced to confront with Joel and Allie on the way here. He could rationalize that they were nearly adults themselves and that this was the way of the post-apocalyptic world in which they now lived. But Bradley and Emma were still young—too young to see a lot of the things that lay ahead or, for that matter, what had happened here today. Of course, this didn't mean he could change any of it or do anything more to protect them from the harsh realities beyond Jack's farm.

Like it or not, Bradley and Emma were going to have to come to terms with all this on their own and in their own time. The best he could do was offer support when he could and be there for them. And as much as it went against his paternal instincts, he needed to be honest with them about all things. At least he would have Sandy to back him up and be another voice of reason.

Ben glanced over at her as she worked the shovel. He could tell that, in better times, she was the type of person who had taken care of herself. She'd come a long way since the FEMA camp rescue. He'd be lying to himself if he said he didn't find her attractive, although he wasn't sure if it was her looks or her attitude that made him feel this way. It was easy to see where Allie's drive and optimistic outlook came from.

In that moment, Ben realized how lucky he was. They'd beaten the odds and, through countless obstacles, made it across the country, where he found his remaining children in good health.

They'd been able to save Allie just in time from God knows what kind of fate in Durango, and they had miraculously found her mother along the way. He considered both of them to be assets to the group. They had all suffered losses, but all in all, they were doing well.

The grave was close to being cleaned out, and Ben was sure there was enough room to properly bury Jack. The grateful feelings he had about their fortune so far began to evaporate with the thought of placing Jack in the hole they had just dug. The time had come, though, and he knew it had to be done now.

Ben briefly considered putting it off until morning but decided against it. He wanted to leave with a clean slate tomorrow, and to him, that seemed unlikely if the first thing they did was bury Jack. At the risk of being callous, he just wanted to get this over with.

"I think it's ready." Ben used the shovel to climb out of the hole, where he joined Allie and her mother on the grass above. Joel kept trying to make it neat and square by trimming pieces of earth from around the edges. The red light of his headlamp cast an eerie glow over the shallow grave, and for some reason, Ben wanted his son to stop digging his grandfather's grave and get up on the grass with them right now.

"Joel, it's done. Come on." Ben stepped to the edge and held out his hand. Joel stopped digging and leaned on his shovel as he looked down at the ground. He didn't say anything but instead let out a deep sigh as he reluctantly took Ben's hand and pulled himself up. Ben couldn't help but think that Joel was trying to stall a little, and he understood.

"Why don't you and Allie see if you can talk them into joining us?" Ben stared back at the house for a moment. "I would do it, but I would rather have the body in the hole and ready when they get here," he added. He wasn't sure why, but he didn't want Bradley and Emma to see him carrying Jack and putting him in the ground.

"Come on." Allie handed Joel a bottle of water and put her arm around him as she pulled him toward the house.

"Thanks, guys." Ben started for the garage but paused. "Don't push them, okay? If they really don't want to be a part of this, it's okay."

Joel looked at his dad for the first time in a while and nodded. None of them wanted to do this, but there was no choice.

· 21 ·

"I'll give you a hand." Sandy hurried to catch up to Ben. As they entered the outbuilding, Ben remembered the other reason why he wanted to get this done tonight. The exhaust pipe for the generator was plumbed through the outside wall and leaked a little. The generator also ran a little rich, so he expected the smell of gas and exhaust fumes, but they were no longer the most offensive odor in the building.

Maybe the stench was more noticeable now because they'd been outside and there was a breeze carrying fresh air from the coast, or maybe the body was decomposing quickly in the heat. The smell would be much worse by morning, and that wasn't how Ben wanted to start the day. The fact that the outbuilding had been completely closed up to muffle the sound of the generator wasn't helping the situation any, either.

Ben threw the tarp back, and the large bloodstain on the comforter caught his eye immediately; he couldn't help but notice it had grown in size. He pulled the tarp back down and wrapped it tightly around the body. There was no point in removing it, and he just wanted to get out of this loud, smelly place as fast as he could. He picked Jack up and carried him outside while Sandy closed the door and locked up behind him. Ben half-jogged to the gravesite and gently but quickly lowered Jack's body into place. He didn't want the kids to come outside while he was doing this and climbed out of the hole as soon as he was done tucking the edges of the tarp neatly underneath the body.

As he and Sandy waited for what he hoped would be all of the kids, Ben began to think about what he was going to say, both to the kids and about Jack, during this impromptu memorial service.

"Do you think it's going to rain soon?" Sandy looked up at the sky as the sound of thunder echoed above. Her question was a welcome interruption to his thoughts.

"It looks like it's getting closer, that's for sure." There were distant flashes of lightning, but the storm seemed to be stalled for the time being.

"Hopefully it'll hold off a little longer." With the grave dug, Ben no longer needed the rain to soften the ground. They were also standing under the only tree around, and except for the house and outbuilding, they were basically in the middle of a large, open field. This wasn't exactly the ideal place to be in a lightning storm.

Ben was about to head inside to see what the holdup was, but he only made it a few steps toward the house when he saw Joel emerge from the back door. Allie was right behind him, followed closely by Bradley and the two dogs. They were all walking slowly, even Gunner and Sam, as if they knew the destination.

"No Emma?" Ben shrugged.

Joel shook his head. "No, she doesn't want to come out."

Ben looked at Sandy. "Maybe I should go talk to her."

"She said she wasn't going to change her mind, even if you came in to talk to her," Allie explained.

Ben sighed as he thought it over. He was hoping they would all participate in this, but at the risk of making this any harder than it already was, he decided to respect Emma's wishes and leave her for the time being. He just hoped she wouldn't come to regret this somewhere down the road.

Everyone gathered around the grave and stared at Jack's tarp-covered body in the hole.

"Would anyone like to say something about Grandpa?" Ben asked.

No one said anything for a few seconds, but it felt more like minutes to Ben as he listened to the not-too-distant thunder.

"I will." Sandy took a half-step forward. "Unfortunately, we didn't get to know Jack for very long, but the short time we had with him was enough to know he was a kind, generous, and caring man that loved his grandchildren dearly. Thank you, Jack, for all you did for us." Sandy wiped away a tear and stepped back.

Allie stepped forward next. "I just wanted to say how grateful I am for him giving us a place to rest and for all the supplies he gave us to help us get home. And I hope he knows that we'll take good care of Sam." Allie fought through her tears as she finished. Sam looked up when she heard her name, and Allie knelt down to give her a hug. Gunner's jealousy got the best of him, and he moved close to Allie's leg, leaning against her and Sam.

When Joel stepped forward, Ben noticed he was holding an old, well-worn Bible.

"I was going to read a Bible verse," Joel said quietly. "I found this Bible on Grandpa's nightstand. There was a bookmark in this page with a couple highlighted verses that seemed pretty fitting to me." He paused for a second and looked at Ben while he tried to keep it together. Ben nodded at him to continue when he was ready. Jack and Carol had been regular churchgoers when she was alive, but as far as Ben knew, Jack had quit attending church after she passed. He hadn't noticed the Bible by Jack's bed. He had to admit that he was caught off guard at Joel's thoughtfulness and maturity in this moment.

"Psalm 46:1-3." Joel cleared his throat, struggling to maintain his composure before continuing. "God is our refuge and strength, an ever-present help in trouble. Therefore we will not fear, though the earth give way and the mountains fall into the heart of the sea, though its waters roar and foam and the mountains quake with their surging."

Joel struggled to get through the last few lines before kneeling and placing the Bible on top of the tarp. Allie was waiting for him when he got up and wrapped her arms around him tightly.

Ben glanced down at Bradley, who was by his side. "Do you want to say anything?" he whispered. Bradley shook his head and pulled in closer to his dad. Ben put his arm around his son and took a deep breath. It was time for him to say something.

"I've known Jack for a long time. We've hunted and fished together a few times over the years, and on those outings, he always talked about family. Your grandpa loved you more than anything else in this world, and I think we can all take a little comfort in knowing that he got to spend his final days with the people he loved the most. Jack gave his life for us, and the best way we can honor him is to keep moving forward. Jack's final words to me were, 'Take care of them.' And that's exactly what I plan on doing. Even in the end, he was only worried about you guys." Ben paused and looked down at the grave. "Thank you, Jack. I won't let you down."

Ben stepped back as he glanced toward the house, hoping to find Emma, but she wasn't anywhere to be seen. They all remained silent for a minute or so before, one by one, they began to back away. Ben walked over to the magnolia tree and took a shovel in his hands.

"I'll take care of the rest if you guys want to head in," Ben said. But before anyone could say anything more, a loud crack of thunder split the air, and the first drops of rain they had seen in over two weeks began to fall. A few large, sporadic drops hit first, sending up small puffs of dust wherever they landed. It quickly turned into a steady drizzle as more thunder rumbled.

"Go ahead, guys. We need to get out from under this tree." Ben raised his voice to compete with the wind and rain.

Everyone but Joel headed for the house. "I can help."

"You don't have to. You practically dug it by yourself. I don't want you to overdo it and be worn out tomorrow. It's going to be a big day and an early start."

"I know. I'm fine." Joel grabbed the other shovel, which was leaning against the tree. Ben didn't want to argue with him right now. He didn't have the energy or the heart, and he wanted to get this done before it turned into mud.

"Do you want to keep the Bible?" Ben asked as they began to shovel dirt into the hole.

"No. I think it was Grandma's. It has pictures of her and all of us in it. I think it should stay with him," Joel answered.

"Okay." Ben felt that it was a mistake to bury the Bible but didn't want to push the issue. They shoveled quickly and quietly for a while as the hard dirt bounced off the tarp and began to fill in the crevices. Joel stopped abruptly and jammed his shovel into the ground, forcing it to stand on its own before he dropped to his knees near the edge of the grave. He frantically reached down and pulled the Bible out of the freshly thrown dirt, then swept his hand across the cover and blew the remaining dirt away with a heavy breath.

"Maybe I should keep it," he stated.

"I think that's a good idea," Ben agreed.

There were still moments when Ben found it hard to believe they were burying Jack, yet here they were, throwing dirt atop a man whom he had come to love and respect. A man who had given his all to ensure the welfare of Bradley and Emma and who, in the end, made the ultimate sacrifice.

With the worsening weather, Ben considered using the tractor to speed up the process and get it over with. If he used it like a plow and pushed the dirt, the landscape box would make quick work of filling in the hole. But that meant taking off the post-hole digger and attaching another implement. By then, it would be a mess out here. Besides, he and Joel were almost halfway done, and somehow, using the tractor felt too cold and uncaring.

The shovelfuls of dirt started to feel heavy as the rain saturated the ground, turning the once-dry earth into mud. Thankfully, the process seemed to go faster once the last pieces of blue tarp disappeared. They rushed to finish as the full brunt of the storm bared down on them now. They were fully soaked as they threw the last few shovels of dirt into the hole. Catching their breath, they both stood there for a second until a bright flash of lightning and a loud clap of thunder prompted them to get moving.

"Come on, let's go." Ben put his hand on Joel's shoulder and pushed him toward the house. They both ran the fifty yards or so back to the house and didn't stop until they were inside and standing in the kitchen. Sandy met them with a warm, fresh towel out of the dryer. It felt cold in the house with the air-conditioner on and their clothes soaked through with rain. Ben inhaled the fresh scent of detergent as he dried his face and head. He couldn't help but let out a sigh of relief. It was done.

· 22 ·

Ben and Joel cleaned up as best as they could with the towels in the kitchen before making their way into the living room. Ben was glad to see Bradley and Emma playing a board game with Allie.

Allie looked them over. "You guys are a mess."

"Yeah, it's really coming down out there," Joel answered.

"Why don't you get cleaned up and I'll do a load of wash?" Sandy said.

"Sounds good." Ben wanted to take Emma aside and talk with her, but she was engrossed in the game and he didn't want to pull her away at the moment. She'd talk when she was ready—at least he hoped she would. It was good to see them all preoccupied with something less serious for a change.

Joel headed upstairs to get cleaned up first while Ben stayed downstairs with the others. He laid his towel across the recliner and took a seat. He felt better running the generator with the storm raging outside. The wind and thunder would do a good job of covering any noise that reached beyond the thin walls of the outbuilding. Besides, he doubted anyone would come out in this weather.

As Ben listened to the heavy rain beat down on the roof, he began to grow tired. It had been a hard day that was both physically and mentally draining. Even with all his concerns about their day tomorrow and the safety of the house tonight, he would have no problem sleeping when it came time. The trucks were loaded except for a few last-minute things, and they had buried Jack. There was nothing else for them to do here except sleep. He felt a sense of relief knowing the day was behind them. Jack's death still hung heavy in the air, but it was different now.

Ben checked the time and ran through the watch schedule in his mind. It was already eight o'clock. The last few hours of the day flew by impossibly fast. He was going to encourage everyone to get a good night's sleep and be in bed by nine. Morning would come quickly, and this was the last night with the comfort of a mattress underneath them for who knew how long.

Sandy would take the first shift tonight and wake Allie up for her turn at midnight until about three in the morning, at which point she'd wake

Ben. He would stand the last watch and stay up through the morning.

He hoped to get on the road by six, but realistically, he'd be happy if they made it out of here by 6:30 or 7:00. They'd have breakfast here, using the generator to power the range and make ice right up until the moment they pulled out.

Joel came down the steps, looking clean and refreshed. "It's all yours."

"All right. I don't see myself making it back downstairs tonight. Everybody good with the watch schedule?" Ben asked. They all nodded.

"Allie, I guess I'll see you around three then. Goodnight, everyone. Don't stay up too late. We're getting an early start tomorrow."

"We won't," Emma answered.

As Ben reached the top of the stairs, he couldn't help but look toward the back bedroom where Jack had died. Fortunately, no one was using that room, and the door could remain closed forever as far as he was concerned. It would be good to move on from this place. They all needed a change of scenery after today's events. Even if they only made it around to the western side of the Chesapeake Bay tomorrow, it would still be progress and a welcome change.

He would have taken a longer shower, but he was more interested in lying down. They'd all have a chance to clean up in the morning one more time before leaving. Right now, the bed was calling his name. Within minutes of lying down, he was out.

The night was uneventful as the rain continued coming down. He only woke once, when Joel had a bad dream and thrashed about wildly in the bed. Ben was able to settle him down quickly, though, and they both fell asleep in minutes. When Allie came to wake him, it hardly seemed possible that the night had passed so quickly. He checked his watch in disbelief and was surprised to see that she had let him sleep until four.

"Thanks," Ben whispered.

"No problem," she answered. "I'll see you downstairs."

Ben dressed quickly and was halfway down the steps when the smell of freshly brewed coffee got his attention. As he entered the kitchen, he saw Allie tending to the coffeemaker on the counter. She turned to face him, holding a cup in her hands.

"Thank you." Ben accepted the steaming mug from Allie and sipped greedily at the hot liquid.

Allie smiled. "I thought you could use that."

Ben nodded and took another sip from the mug before setting it down at the kitchen table.

"You should try to get a little more sleep before we leave. We still have a couple hours."

"Yeah, I think I'm going to try to do that." Allie started for the stairs.

"Hey, Allie?"

"Yeah?"

"Thanks for everything. I mean, for taking time to talk with Emma and everything else you do to help out. I'm really glad you and your mom are with us."

Allie's face turned red as she blushed and smiled again. "I'm glad we're here, too." Allie spoke quietly and then disappeared up the staircase. Ben sat down at the kitchen table to drink his coffee and put his boots on. For the first time since Allie woke him, he realized that the rain had stopped. He finished putting his boots on and topped off his cup of coffee before heading to the back door.

As the door slowly creaked open, Ben heard Gunner and Sam bounding down the steps. They were anxious to go outside, and Sam impatiently forced the door open with her nose as soon as she reached it. Both dogs cleared the porch in seconds and hit the yard running, only slowing down occasionally to sniff the wet grass.

Ben picked up the AR-15 with the Trijicon optic and followed the dogs out as far as the porch, where he stayed and savored the coffee. Keeping an eye on the dogs, he surveyed the surrounding fields. The sky was noticeably clearer, and the moon cast a dim light over the neat rows of soybeans. Any signs of the storm and the dark clouds that came with it were long gone. He looked up at the sky and could actually see the stars. It had been a long time since he'd seen the sky this clear. The foggy haze they'd grown accustomed to was nowhere to be seen. As he drew in a deep breath of fresh air, he wondered if this might be the beginning of a return to normal, at least as far as the weather was concerned.

He joined the dogs in the yard, and they followed him as he made a quick perimeter check and walked around the house. Satisfied that all was quiet, he headed back inside for more coffee and a comfortable place to sit while he waited for the sun to rise.

The dogs seemed content to stay downstairs with him, and both were soon fast asleep on the living room floor. Wide awake after his third cup of coffee, Ben sat in the recliner and decided to do something he'd been putting off since Jack died yesterday. It wasn't something he was looking forward to, but it needed to be done: he needed to leave a letter for Casey in case she actually made it back here.

She was likely dead, although he would never share that opinion with the kids, but he felt compelled to write at least a basic note letting her know where the kids were. He'd want her to do the same for him if their roles were reversed. If nothing else, it would make the kids feel better about leaving. He found a tablet and pencil in one of the drawers and cleared a spot at the kitchen table.

After staring at the blank sheet of paper for what felt like forever, he eventually decided what to say and began to write.

Casey,

First things first, Bradley, Emma, and Joel are safe with me and headed to Colorado. When we arrived, your dad was in poor health but had taken good care of Bradley and Emma. He put all he had into taking care of the kids and sadly passed the day after we arrived. We buried him under the magnolia tree as per his request.

I can take care of the kids better at home than I can here. I hope you understand, but I have to do what's best for them. We left for Colorado on June 21st. If you have the means, you are more than welcome to join us. If things ever return to normal, I'll do my best to contact you.

Stay safe,
Ben

P.S. Sam is with us and we have your dad's Jeep.

Ben read the letter over a few times and decided to let it go at that. It was short and to the point. He didn't feel the need to go into detail about how Jack died or what had happened. He was still angry with her for leaving the kids here with Jack in the first place. If she found her way back and read the letter, she would know the kids were safe and where they were. What else was there to say?

He tore the sheet off the tablet and folded it neatly before writing her name on the outside and attaching it to the refrigerator with a magnet. He couldn't help but feel it was a waste of time, but at least his conscience was clear and he had done what he could. If he was being honest, he did it more as a good-faith gesture for the kids' sake. If they saw that he'd left their mother a letter, maybe it would help ease their minds and give them hope for her safe return from wherever she was.

· 23 ·

With the letter to his ex done and a little guilt off his chest, Ben decided to focus on making ice and packing up as much venison as he could. They were taking two small, well-insulated coolers they found in the garage. Ben's plan was to layer the meat between ice and newspaper to keep it frozen for as long as possible. He was hoping the newspaper would provide enough insulation to get an extra day or two out of the venison. He wasn't sure if it would make a difference, but it was worth a try.

Ben shook his head at the thought of having to leave some of the venison behind, but they were pushing it by adding the two coolers to their load-out. He hated the thought of leaving anything of value behind, but there were limits to what they could carry.

The thought of ditching the Jeep for the Chevy pickup the two men were driving had crossed his mind, but the pickup was only two-wheel drive and he wasn't sure what kind of mechanical condition it was in. While going through the pickup for anything useful, he'd noticed that the restoration seemed to be mostly cosmetic. At least he knew the condition of the Jeep; if Jack said it was in good shape and that he'd fixed everything mechanical, Ben had no reason to think otherwise. Jack wasn't the type of person to skimp on something like that.

The first thing Ben did was turn off the generator. Everyone was sleeping, and the house was plenty cool for now. He'd fire it back up when he was done in the garage. Fortunately, he could only smell exhaust in the garage. He opened up the overhead doors to help air the place out. Thanks to the generator running all night, he could barely breathe in here.

While the fumes dissipated, Ben stood outside for a while and enjoyed the fresh, clean air the storm left behind. The eastern horizon was already beginning to show signs of a soon-to-be-rising sun. He checked his watch and found it hard to believe that it was almost five already. The morning had flown by so far, and the thought of getting into the trucks and driving out of here seemed very real all of a sudden. It was what he wanted, but it gave him anxiety nonetheless.

Ben watched Gunner and Sam for a few more minutes while he waited for the outbuilding to clear out. The dogs were busy patrolling the yard and inspecting every inch as if they had never seen it before. He couldn't help but think about how happy they were to have fresh air as well. The others would also be pleasantly surprised to wake up to this welcome change.

As the sun began to creep over the horizon, Ben noticed the lack of smoke plumes, something else that had become part of the normal landscape. Whatever small, smoldering fires remained had been put out by the downpour. Ben hoped the rest of the country would begin to normalize. Every place they had passed through on the way here could benefit greatly from a storm like the one that rolled through here last night.

A few minutes had passed since he opened the big overhead doors of the outbuilding, so he headed inside to see if he could tolerate the smell enough to load the coolers. It still reeked of unburnt fuel, but the haze floating near the ceiling when he first walked in was gone.

He began meticulously loading the coolers with the paper-wrapped packages of meat. He was careful to place each one so that the next package would fit neatly next to it and take up as little space as possible. It was a little like putting a puzzle together without knowing what it was supposed to look like. Every time he made an even layer of venison, he topped it off with a layer of ice and newspaper before starting with the meat again. He repeated this process until both coolers were tightly packed. Then he finished them off by stuffing fresh ice from the icemaker into the cracks and crevices between the meat. He secured one of the cooler's lids with duct tape to ensure that it remained closed with a good seal until they used all the meat from the first one.

Ben glanced at his watch again to check the time. He wanted to start getting everyone up around 5:30. He had a few more minutes to kill, so he decided to at least secure one of the coolers in place before he went back inside. He lashed the taped-up cooler in place to the rear rack on the Blazer with several bungee cords. Stepping back, he looked at the already loaded-down Jeep and wondered where the other cooler would go. He checked his watch again and decided to worry about that later.

He'd let the others sleep in long enough. It was almost a quarter to six, and it was time for everyone to get moving. Before heading in, he searched the chest freezer for a suitable piece of venison to cook for breakfast. He settled on a large pack of meat. It was more than they would have normally used for one meal, but there was no point in saving what remained.

He felt bad about leaving behind what he couldn't squeeze into the coolers and decided to pull out another pack of steaks for the dogs. Gunner and Sam seemed to sense his intentions and came running at the sound of the freezer lid slamming shut.

"Oh, you think you're getting something, huh?" Ben joked as the dogs anxiously circled him like two hungry sharks. He might as well give it to them now, while it was still frozen. They'd be occupied for the remainder of the morning or at the very least until it was time to go.

Both dogs began to whine and pace nervously as he unwrapped the steaks. Sam took hers gently, as if she was doing something wrong, but once she had it in her mouth, her tail began to wag furiously. She quickly found her dog bed and lay down just a few feet away from Ben. Gunner latched onto the steak with less caution than Sam and let out a low, playful growl as he passed by the older dog and retreated to the far corner of the outbuilding with his prize.

Ben headed for the house with the other pack of venison. He considered locking everything up and making the dogs come inside but decided to leave things as they were. He'd be right back after he woke everyone up, and the dogs would keep an eye on things for a few minutes while he was gone. When he came back, he planned on moving the trucks outside and closing everything up so they could run the generator quietly for the last hour or so that they were here. If anyone approached the property, the dogs would bark and alert him.

When he entered the house, he was surprised to see Joel in the kitchen. He was pouring the last of the coffee into a mug and looked like he was still half asleep.

"Morning," Ben said.

"Morning," Joel mumbled. "Hey, I tried to take a shower, but the water isn't working."

"Yeah, I've got the generator off right now. I was working in the garage. Gunner and Sam are out there with me, too. I was just bringing this inside, then heading back out." Ben tossed the meat onto the counter.

Joel eyed the neatly wrapped package. "That's a lot. You want to cook all that for breakfast?" he asked.

"Might as well. I've got the coolers maxed out. We can't take any more with us unfortunately."

"That sucks," Joel grumbled.

Ben smiled. "Gunner and Sam would disagree. They're outside enjoying frozen deer steaks right now."

Joel parted the curtain and looked out the kitchen window. "They must have finished them because they're both standing in the yard right now."

"That's impossible." Ben wrinkled his brow. Gunner was a powerful chewer and usually made quick work of any treats or bones that came his way, but even for him, that was fast. The steaks were practically frozen solid when he handed them to the dogs. Ben took a couple of steps toward the door and peeked outside. Joel was right: the dogs were both standing in the yard and looking out toward the road. From where they were, they couldn't see down the driveway, but something had their attention. Ben's pulse quickened as he heard the familiar sound of gravel crunching under tires. Someone was coming!

· 24 ·

"Get the others up and wait inside until I see what's going on." Ben picked up the AR-15 from where he had leaned it against the wall by the back door.

Joel was wide awake now. "I can help."

Ben glanced back at him. "No, I need you to get the others up and stay inside. You can keep an eye on things from the window. Just be ready if I need you. The KSG is by the steps."

Joel sighed. "Okay."

He looked disappointed, but the others needed to be woken up and told what was going on, and there was no time for any further discussion. Joel might not have been happy about it, but Ben was glad to see him drop it and head out of the kitchen to warn the others.

Ben crossed the deck and flew down the steps in a matter of seconds. Both dogs were standing just past the corner of the house now and were out in the middle of the driveway so they could see the road. Ben couldn't hear the vehicle, but there was no doubt that someone was coming. Gunner's hackles were up, and he was growling loudly. It was a low, guttural rumble that Ben had heard many times before. Sam was also doing her part by barking aggressively at whoever was approaching. Ben let them go. He was actually thankful for the distraction they were providing. With them blocking the driveway and carrying on like that, whoever this was would initially be focused on the dogs, giving Ben a chance to inch his head around the corner of the house to get a look.

The old black Dodge pickup crept along at a ridiculously slow speed, giving Ben plenty of time to spy on its occupants through the ACOG scope. It was an older couple who looked to be around the same age as Jack. They appeared harmless, but Ben wasn't about to let his guard down, no matter how innocent they seemed. They were too close to leaving now, and he didn't want anything to interfere with their plans.

Maybe they were Jack's friends coming to check on him; at least that was what Ben hoped, so he kept the AR trained on the truck. When the truck neared, Ben decided it wasn't a good idea to have the dogs out on the open gravel lane. If the couple was up to no good, they could easily dispatch the dogs by simply running them down.

"Gunner... Sam. Come here," Ben said sternly. Gunner looked in his direction but stood his ground against the approaching truck. Sam followed suit and only briefly acknowledged Ben with a quick glance before she returned to bellowing out her warning at the intruders.

"Gunner, heal up!" Ben demanded. Gunner took a few steps toward the house, but after realizing that Sam wasn't moving, he stopped and resumed his growling.

The truck hadn't picked up speed, but it showed no signs of slowing, either. Ben didn't need the scope to see the occupants clearly now, and he knew it was time to take action. Keeping the butt of the AR firmly seated against his shoulder, he slowly stepped out into the driveway. The truck stopped abruptly about twenty yards away. Both the driver and the passenger raised their hands to where they could be easily seen.

Ben began to walk backward and move off the driveway as he waved them forward with the gun. He kept the AR trained on the driver as they began creeping forward again. The dogs followed him as he moved off the gravel lane and into the grass.

The brakes squeaked as the Dodge came to a stop, and the man driving made a motion with his hand to indicate that he wanted to roll the window down. Ben nodded his approval but kept the gun ready.

"Sam, Gunner, easy." Ben tried to quiet the dogs while the man cranked the window down a few inches.

"We're friends of Jack's. I'm Charlie Smith and this is my wife, Alice."

Ben lowered the gun and relaxed his stance but still kept the barrel pointed at the truck. Jack had mentioned that the Smiths were taking care of him and that they were going to bury him under the tree when the time came. The man turned the truck off and climbed out.

As Charlie exited the vehicle, Sam's demeanor changed immediately, and her tail began to wag. Gunner continued growling softly, but his tail was wagging now, too. Charlie still had his hands up halfway as he took a step away from the truck and looked at the outbuilding and the trucks parked inside. Ben noticed the handgun on Charlie's hip. The large revolver barely fit in the holster.

"You must be Ben," Charlie said. Ben lowered the gun all the way to his side and stuck his hand out.

"That's right. Nice to meet you, Charlie. Sorry about the greeting, but you can't be too careful these days."

"Oh, no problem. Believe me, I understand." His wife was out of the truck now and joined them. She was carrying a small basket with a cloth covering the top of it. Gunner and Sam went straight for the basket and gave it a good going-over with their noses. Gunner was no longer growling and instead seemed to only care about what was inside.

"Hi, Sam." The woman gave Sam a few pats on the head. "And who's your friend?" She bent down and scratched Gunner's neck before turning her attention to Ben.

"Hi, I'm Alice."

"Hi there. That's Gunner," Ben said.

"We were just stopping by to check on Jack and the kids. How's he doing?" Charlie asked.

Ben looked at Alice and then back at Charlie as he shook his head. "Yesterday." Ben stepped aside and looked across the yard toward the magnolia tree.

"Oh dear." Alice teared up as Charlie pulled her close.

He sighed. "We knew it wouldn't be long, but that's a lot sooner than I expected."

Alice sniffed. "Poor Jack. He was a good man. It's a good thing you got here when you did, for the kids' sake. We offered to have the kids come stay with us. Jack, too, for that matter, but he wouldn't have it."

"He had a feeling you'd be coming for the kids. When did you get in?" Charlie asked.

"Couple days ago," Ben answered.

"Colorado, right?" Charlie began walking toward the magnolia tree.

"Yeah, it took longer than I wanted to get here, but as you can imagine, we ran into our share of trouble on the way here." Ben followed Charlie and Alice as they made their way to Jack's grave.

Joel appeared on the deck. "Everything okay out here?" He held the KSG loosely at his side.

"Yeah, it's the Smiths. They're friends of your grandpa's."

"And you must be Joel. We've heard a lot about you." Alice changed course and started for the deck.

Charlie followed and shook Joel's hand as he came down the steps. "You're a lot bigger than the pictures your grandfather showed us. He talked about you a lot. Your grandfather was a good man and a close friend of ours."

One by one, the others filed out of the house and onto the deck. Everyone introduced themselves, and eventually, they wound up back inside and sitting around the kitchen table. Ben was pleased to see that Alice was carrying eggs in the basket and invited them to stay for breakfast. It would delay their departure by a few minutes, but it was the least he could do for the couple.

They were nice people, and that was a rare commodity these days. Besides, they were partially responsible for the welfare of Bradley and Emma. Through the course of the conversation, Ben learned that Charlie and Alice had stopped in to check on Jack and the kids every couple of days, bringing them eggs and occasionally baked goods when they could. They had risked their safety and shared their limited resources to ensure that the kids were well-fed and taken care of.

Ben was more than happy to give the Smiths the remainder of the venison from the chest freezer. It did his heart good to know that the meat wouldn't go to waste. He also made sure to give Charlie the hunting rifle that Jack wanted him to have, and he encouraged them to take whatever else they thought they could use from the house or garage.

After breakfast, they made their way out to the grave—all except Emma, who still refused to go anywhere near it. Charlie and Alice paid their respects to Jack and promised to keep an eye out for Casey if she returned. That seemed to make the kids happy and maybe made the possibility of their mother being all right more believable.

They talked for a while longer as Ben helped Charlie load his truck with the remaining deer meat and a few other things he thought they could use from the garage. They said their goodbyes and wished Ben and the others safe travels.

The encounter with the Smiths was bittersweet and left Ben feeling a little guilty. Here was a couple that was willing to go out of their way to help them, and all he could offer them in exchange were a few meager supplies. They weren't young by any means and long past their prime. How much longer would this kind couple be able to hold out against the trials and hardships that surely lay ahead?

· 25 ·

Ben checked his watch as the old Dodge pulled onto the paved road and disappeared out of sight. It was 6:30, and although he hoped to be on the road by now, he had no regrets about taking the extra time with the Smiths. He hoped they could hang on until things improved or help arrived in some form or another.

Everyone sprung into action as soon as they were gone. There wasn't much left to do except pack up their personal bags and a few odds and ends. Joel helped Ben move the trucks onto the gravel parking area in front of the outbuilding while the others did a last-minute walk-through of the house.

The kids took a few minutes to write personal notes for their mother and put them up on the refrigerator next to Ben's. Emma also insisted that they leave a small bag of groceries filled with non-perishable items on the counter for their mother's sake. Ben knew it was a waste of valuable resources and would most likely end up in the hands of the next looters who came through, but it wasn't worth the argument. Right now, Emma needed all the hope he could give her.

She still hadn't been out to the grave, and Ben was worried that she would regret that somewhere down the road when they were too far away to do anything about it. He didn't want to push too much, though. They had all been through a lot, and it was hard knowing what was going through the kids' minds right now. The journey ahead was going to be long and grueling; being on bad terms with his daughter wasn't how he wanted to start the trip.

Somehow, Joel found time to fashion a rough wooden cross from a couple of wood scraps he found in the outbuilding. All the kids wrote something small on the cross to honor Jack's memory, and Ben was relieved to see Emma at least participate in that.

She'd come around on her own when she was ready. At least that was what he told himself. It wasn't for his lack of trying to get through to her. On more than one occasion since Jack died, he'd tried to no avail to get her to open up and talk. Allie and Sandy had even given it a shot, too, but she seemed content to keep to herself for now.

Earlier, Charlie had said a small prayer for all of them when they gathered around the Dodge to say farewell, and Ben recalled some of the words. In addition to asking for traveling mercies as they crossed the country, Charlie said something that resonated with Ben. He asked that they all be given strength to face down whatever obstacles they might encounter along the way. Ben wondered if knowing when to be silent and letting the kids work things out in their own time was part of that strength.

Bradley seemed to be taking things in stride and was content to follow his big brother around, helping wherever he could. Joel was eager to play the role and appeared happy, considering the situation. He enthusiastically took Bradley under his wing.

It was good to have the kids together again, and in a way, Ben felt that, regardless of what happened from here on out, he had already succeeded in some small way as far as the kids were concerned. They would draw strength from each other, and that would do a great deal when it came to maintaining morale in the tough moments they would certainly encounter.

In that moment, Ben was overcome with the feeling that if he could get them back home to Durango, life would be okay again. Maybe not right away, and probably not in a way any of them would consider normal, but it would be better. It was something to focus on right now, and that was all the reason he needed to keep moving forward, no matter what obstacles lay ahead.

On one of Joel's trips out of the house to the Jeep, Ben noticed he had a small bundle made of a bathroom towel. He caught his dad looking and pulled a piece of the towel back to reveal Jack's ornate .45 and leather holster.

Ben expected to see him wearing the gun, but Joel said he wanted to make sure it stayed in good condition. He was worried about scratching it and gently tucked it under the Jeep's front driver's seat, along with a few boxes of ammunition, just in case.

The trip would be different this time with two vehicles. He didn't like the idea of being separated from Joel and Allie, but there was no way around it. They had the two-way radios, but Ben thought it would be wise to establish some basic hand signals.

He planned on always being close enough that a hand signal out the window could be easily seen between the Blazer and the Jeep. Plus, they could avoid using the battery-powered radios for basic communication and save them for emergencies and times when they needed to talk in detail.

He went over the signals with everyone and made sure they all understood what they meant. It was important that they all knew how to communicate, not just the people who would be driving. A closed fist meant that Ben was stopping the truck. Holding his hand flat with the palm down meant that he was preparing to slow down. A wave of the hand with a forward motion meant he wanted Joel to pull up alongside him. Two fingers pointing forward indicated that there was something ahead. If Ben put his arm out the window and tapped the door with his hand, that would be the signal to let them know they needed to stop for fuel soon. Last but not least, a closed fist with the thumb and pinky extended in the shape of a phone would be the cue to use the two-way radio. After that, they could use their fingers to indicate which channel to use if channel six, the one they agreed to leave the radios on, wasn't clear.

With the packing complete and all things triple-checked, there was nothing more they could do to prepare. It was time to go. Ben hesitated as he closed the door to the house, taking a second to look back inside. There was a good chance they would never be here again. The bag of food on the counter caught his eye, and he thought about Casey. He really did hope she was okay and that she would make it back.

Everyone gathered around the trucks, and Gunner was the first to load up. He was anxious to go for a ride and blissfully unaware of the many miles ahead of them. He had obviously forgotten about all the long hours spent cooped up in the Blazer just a couple of short days ago. Ben did a quick headcount and realized that Emma and Sam were missing. His heart skipped a beat as he searched the yard. Was she still inside? Maybe he'd missed her when he did his last walk-through of the house. How did he not notice she wasn't among them? He'd been too preoccupied with making sure the trucks were well-packed and ready.

"Where's Emma?" Ben asked. Everyone stopped what they were doing and looked around.

"There she is." Bradley pointed. Ben was surprised to see his daughter kneeling next to the grave. Sam was sitting next to her in the shadow of the magnolia tree; she had her arm around the dog as they sat there in silence.

"Do you want me to go and get her?" Joel asked.

"No, let her be." Ben was proud of her for being brave, and even though he was anxious to leave, he would have waited all day if that was what it took to make her happy. But they didn't have to wait long. Within a few minutes, Emma rose to her feet. At first, she headed away from them, and Ben started to grow nervous until he realized that she was picking a few weeds that resembled flowers. She laid them near the cross marker that Joel had made and then headed back toward the group. Sam lingered for a few seconds longer and finally followed after Emma called out to her. Ben wondered if the old dog somehow understood the finality of the moment.

Emma walked over to her dad and forced a crooked smile. "I'm ready to go now." She gave him a quick hug and matter-of-factly headed for the Blazer.

The time had come to leave Jack's behind, and as everyone loaded up and prepared to pull out, Ben found it hard to believe that they were actually leaving after fighting so hard to get here. There was a lot of road between them and Durango, but he took comfort in the fact that they were finally heading home.

Find out about Bruno Miller's next book by signing
up for his newsletter:
http://brunomillerauthor.com/sign-up/

No spam, no junk, just news (sales, freebies, and
releases). Scouts honor.

Enjoy the book?
Help the series grow by telling a friend about it
and taking the time to leave a review.

BOOKS BY BRUNO MILLER

THE DARK ROAD SERIES:
Breakdown
Escape
Resistance
Fallout
Extraction
Reckoning

CLOVERDALE SERIES:
Impact
Survival
Endurance

ABOUT THE AUTHOR

BRUNO MILLER is the author of the Dark Road series. He's a military vet who likes to spend his downtime hanging out with his wife and kids, or getting in some range time. He believes in being prepared for any situation.

http://brunomillerauthor.com/

https://www.facebook.com/BrunoMillerAuthor/